"Listen, Shane."

Lexi jabbed at his chest. "Regardless of how or what I feel, you cannot kiss me while I'm at work, even if you do own the place! Who knows who saw that kiss? I have a reputation to maintain, so I suggest you get your butt on that plane and focus on your next ride."

"After you admit you still love me." Shane leisurely leaned against the stall door.

Lexi closed the distance between them and carefully kept her tone low so no one would overhear. "You arrogant, egotistical— How can you think for one minute— We just started—"

"Yep, I knew it." Shane slapped his thigh with his hat. "Some things never change, *mi ángel de fuego.*"

Taking her off guard, Lexi was surprised to hear Shane refer to her as his "angel of fire." The last time she'd heard the nickname was before they broke up. Struggling to compose herself she stared at him, afraid to speak.

"Whenever you get riled up like this and can't finish a thought, I know I'm right, and it kills you," he said.

If he only knew how much it all really was killing her....

Dear Reader,

Blame It on the Rodeo brings me back to when I interned on a horse ranch in New Jersey many years ago. My job of assisting the breed manager was far from easy, but the rewards outweighed the mud, muck and, well, all those other horse hind-end things. When I wrote this book, I was sad to discover the place that taught me so much no longer exists. While the people and foals I grew to love have moved on to greener pastures, the memories of those days come to life again in this book and the entire Ramblewood series.

I would like to thank Ashleigh Orrock of Seaside Animal Care in Calabash, North Carolina, for inspiring my opening scene. A passing conversation during an emergency vet visit led to the first chapter of this book and began the bumpy trail ride of Lexi and Shane's reconnection.

Blame It on the Rodeo is the third book in the Ramblewood, Texas series, where the Langtry men always manage to rile up the women they love more than a yellow jacket in an outhouse.

Feel free to stop in and visit me at www.amandarenee.com. I'd love to hear from you. Happy reading!

Amanda Renee

BLAME IT ON THE RODEO

—

AMANDA RENEE

HARLEQUIN® AMERICAN ROMANCE®

Recycling programs
for this product may
not exist in your area.

ISBN-13: 978-0-373-75508-0

BLAME IT ON THE RODEO

Printed in U.S.A.

ABOUT THE AUTHOR

Born and raised in the northeast, Amanda Renee currently resides on the Intracoastal Waterway in sunny South Carolina. Her dreams came true when she was discovered through Harlequin's So You Think You Can Write contest.

When not creating stories about love, laughter and things that go bump in the night, she enjoys the company of her schnoodle named Duffy, traveling, photography, playing guitar and anything involving horses. You can visit her at www.amandarenee.com.

Books by Amanda Renee

HARLEQUIN AMERICAN ROMANCE

1442—BETTING ON TEXAS
1464—HOME TO THE COWBOY

For Susan Gibbs Woods

Friends Forever Girlie—'Til we meet again in heaven

Chapter One

"Let's see if we can catch us a foal."

Sliding her arm into the sterile shoulder-length glove, Lexi Lawson slipped the neck strap over her head and faced Little Miss Confetti.

"Easy, girl." Billy Stevens led the white-and-black American Paint mare into the narrow wooden-and-metal crush and closed the front gate. The secured enclosure protected Lexi from the horse and the horse from itself during the procedure. Standing to the side, Billy whispered soothing words while gently rubbing Confetti's muzzle.

"Welcome to your first embryo transfer lesson—so come on back here for a ringside seat." Amused by Billy's stunned expression, she continued, "Equine care starts at conception, and there's more to horses than leg wraps and Coggins reports." Lexi was pleased at how proficient her protégé had become at aiding her with the standard Equine Infectious Anemia tests and the subsequent paperwork.

A year and a half ago Lexi wouldn't have considered Billy Stevens for an assistant. After escaping his abusive family, Billy ended up on the wrong side of the law when he and a few so-called friends stole some high-priced guitars from Ackerman's Music in town. A month in county lockup left him scared straight and completely alone once he was released. Never ones to turn away a person in need, the Langtry family offered him a place to live on the Bridle Dance Ranch in exchange for honest, hard work.

Cole, the oldest of the four Langtry brothers, took a shine to Billy when he noticed his interest in horses ran deeper than a paycheck. Without confidence in himself, Billy didn't believe he had a future in the veterinary field until Cole pointed him in Lexi's direction and offered to help finance some college courses this past semester. A natural, Billy instinctively sensed when a horse was even the slightest bit off.

"We'll be successful today," Ashleigh assured them.

Billy bashfully squeezed past Ashleigh and the crush. Lexi suspected he had a case of puppy love for her vet tech, but he'd soon come to realize no matter how endearing he might be, Ashleigh wasn't about to leave her husband for someone seven years her junior.

"Cole," Lexi said over her shoulder. "Have one of the grooms on standby to bring in Moonglow."

Before Cole answered, Shane Langtry cleared his throat in the doorway of the breeding area and casually leaned against the jamb.

"I'm headed out to pick up our first official rodeo student." Shane straightened and strode over to the mare and stroked her cheek. Responding to his gentle touch, she snorted against his hand and bobbed her head.

Dressed in faded jeans and a formfitting, ab-enhancing fitted gray T-shirt, Shane shouldn't make her breath catch, but damned if he didn't, even after thirteen years. Lexi may have put his cheating ways in the past, but no one said working near the man responsible for the toughest decision of her life would be easy. Of course, she had the option to start over somewhere else, and she'd done just that for a spell.

After a year at Colorado State, Lexi transferred to Cornell University in Ithaca, New York, where she completed veterinary school and her equine internship. She'd been set to stay in the upstate area, but Joe Langtry's call six months later with a job offer and the opportunity to branch out on her own was impossible to resist. The Langtry patriarch was a true Southern charmer who had a way with words, and the money sure didn't hurt, either.

While it was an adjustment from the bone-chilling northern winters, once Lexi moved back to her family's farm, she knew Ramblewood, Texas, would always be home. Regrets were a waste of time and Lexi wasn't about to let a moment pass her by. Jumping into the swing of things with her old friends, she learned to adjust to having Shane in her life again, but it wasn't until his brother Jesse's wedding last November that she and Shane had started chipping away at the pain of the past. Some memories may have faded, but one still haunted her.

"You've been waiting for this day for a long time." Lexi smiled up at Shane. "I wish you the best."

Needing to concentrate on Little Miss Confetti, Lexi shifted her attention away from the roguish cowboy. After administering lidocaine to relax the mare's hindquarters, Ashleigh wrapped its tail in pink, stretchy bandaging and loosely tied it to the crush's back-gate support.

"Most important—everything must be sterile," Lexi explained to Billy. In her peripheral vision, she noticed

Shane still watching her, making her acutely aware how many people banked on her success today. "We don't want any unnecessary risk of infection."

"I still don't understand," Billy said. "Why are we using a surrogate if Confetti's already pregnant?"

"She's our top cutting-horse competitor," Cole said. "Eleven months is too long to keep her out of the ring, and then we'd have to retrain and get her endurance levels up to par again. When she's older and no longer competing, we'll allow her to carry."

"Plus we can get two foals from Confetti this year if we use a surrogate." Lexi had read how some veterinarians were transferring up to six embryos a year from their donor mares by constantly manipulating their heat cycles. She didn't agree with the practice and was glad the Langtrys were equally opposed to it. She only dared so much when it came to messing around with Mother Nature. "We also use surrogates if there's an injury and the horse can't carry to term, or if there are problems due to a previous pregnancy. There are many reasons, but we make sure overbreeding isn't one of them."

Billy's eyes darted between the equipment and the mare. "Will this hurt her?"

"It may feel a little strange to her, but there's no pain," Lexi reassured him. "The process goes very quickly. Mystified Moonglow is our surrogate, but we had to prepare more than one mare in case she didn't ovulate the prerequisite two days after Confetti. The ultrasound shows we're right on schedule with both horses."

Ashleigh placed a white tube in Lexi's free hand. "This is a two-way catheter," Lexi said, turning her wrist over. "Ashleigh will attach one channel to the embryo flush."

Carefully inserting the catheter, Lexi inflated the bulb inside Confetti's cervix to prevent the flush from flowing out while Ashleigh connected the saline solution with long tubing and elevated it on a modified IV stand above Confetti's backside.

"Embryo collection is always done on day seven or eight after ovulation," she explained. "At six days, it's not quite viable, and once we reach the nine-day mark, the embryo is too large and we risk damaging it. Day eight is perfect, and once we know where it is in the petri dish, it will be visible to the naked eye."

"I hope this works," Cole said. "What's the saying, third time's the charm?"

"It's also the last," Lexi stated flatly. If she failed again, she would know this wasn't meant to be, and she didn't want to tempt fate.

"This isn't foolproof. We're looking at a fifty-to-seventy percent success rate. I've always collected them on the second go-round, if we missed the first, but Confetti's been my problem child."

Lexi released a small amount of fluid through the tube and into the horse. Opening the switch between the two channels, the solution flowed through the other side of the tubing and into a filter cup that Ashleigh held.

"The trick is to always have some fluid in the cup, never allowing it to drain all the way into the bucket," Ashleigh added. "We don't want the embryo to smack hard against the side of the cup on its way out."

A few minutes later, Lexi removed the catheter and transferred the collection cup to the Langtrys' lab area. None of her other patients had their own laboratories, but then none of them owned one of the state's largest paint and quarter cutting horse ranches.

Lexi was grateful that Joe Langtry had spared no expense when he built the facility, because it allowed her greater opportunities to expand her knowledge while working in the field.

A bead of sweat traveled down between her shoulder blades in spite of the room's cool climate-controlled air. Opening a grid-lined petri dish, Lexi meticulously poured the contents of the cup into it and turned on the microscope.

"We're using the stereo microscope today." She peered into the eyepiece and adjusted the focus knob. "Examining the cells in three dimensions allows me to grade the quality of the embryo."

Slowly moving the dish under the microscope, she scanned the solution, grid by grid, hoping they wouldn't come up empty again.

"We're in luck, folks." Lexi let out the breath she'd been holding since she arrived on the Bridle Dance Ranch that morning and smiled. "Cole, can you have someone return Confetti to her stall and move Moonglow into the crush? Ashleigh will prep her.

"Take a look." Lexi slid over, making room for Billy, who hovered nearby. "We have a grade one embryo. See how the cells are compacted and all the same size? That's what we always look for."

A lot rode on this dream match between dam Little Miss Confetti and sire Dreamward Wink. The buyer, Blueford Thomas, was a longtime family friend, but Lexi had the feeling everyone was beginning to doubt her ability to get the job done, including Shane.

Seemingly satisfied, Shane turned and left the lab area without a word. Knowing full well this situation was different, Lexi couldn't help but think of the day he'd walked out on her so long ago. Ironically, an unborn child was involved, too.

"Let's transfer this baby into its new home for the next eleven months."

SHANE CURSED HIMSELF on his way out of the stables. Damned if the sight of her didn't still make his blood boil. It had taken a few years after she returned home for Lexi to warm up to Shane, but she still kept him at arm's length. And who'd blame her? The one time he'd cheated on her led to a two-year nightmare he'd rather forget.

A couple days before Lexi came home for winter break from Colorado State, buckle bunny Sharon Vincent knocked on his door and claimed she was five months pregnant with his kid. Their one night in Oklahoma shortly after high school graduation came back to bite him in the ass. Sharon wasn't just bad news when he met her, she was a hot mess and Shane didn't have the good sense to resist. Claiming she was on the pill, he'd learned the hard way not to trust a woman in the birth control department.

Pressured by his family to do the right thing, he immediately married Sharon, breaking Lexi's heart in the process. He'd never forget the afternoon he told Lexi the truth. Her hazel eyes flared at him like a cougar ready to attack. Only she didn't say a word. He had no choice but to walk away from her and they'd kept their distance from one another until his father enticed her to return to town permanently. Shane knew it was for his benefit. Joe Langtry loved to control situations and Shane believed his father thought he and Lexi would one day take another stab at what they'd lost.

Shane married Sharon, and for their son Dylan's sake

he kept up the facade even though he didn't love his wife. Shortly after Dylan's first birthday, Tab Fanning, Shane's biggest rodeo rival, rode into town and turned his world upside down when he claimed to be Dylan's father.

Shane hadn't wanted to believe the child he'd grown to love wasn't his, and Sharon fed him lie after lie, swearing Dylan was his son. He convinced himself that it didn't matter. He loved Dylan and at this point didn't care who the father was, until a court-ordered paternity test proved otherwise. Shattered when Tab took Dylan away, Shane immediately sent Sharon packing.

Before walking out the door, Sharon admitted she had only wanted the Langtry money and had intended to get pregnant that lone night with Shane. Her fatal flaw was sleeping with one too many cowboys around the same time. It took every ounce of Shane's strength and that of his brothers not to strangle her on the spot. From that day forward, Shane declared marriage and children off-limits.

Throwing himself into the rodeo and his work on the ranch kept his mind busy and there was no shortage of women to occupy his bed at night. His romantic relationship with Lexi was in the past but the memory of what they'd had plagued him.

They worked together, ran in the same circles and were usually found in the same places after the sun went down, but until Jesse's wedding, Shane wouldn't have even considered the possibility of a second chance. Maybe it was the clever way Miranda, Jesse's wife, paired them together during the ceremony and reception. Or, maybe it was the sight of Lexi in her beaded sage bridesmaid gown. Whatever the reason, the moment she took his arm during the wedding procession, Shane knew where his heart belonged—where it had never left.

"There's my elusive son," his mother greeted him on the dirt path leading to the stables. "I haven't seen you in two days. Thought I'd take a break from the ribbon-cutting preparations and see how Lexi made out." Kay peered up at him. "Have you heard anything yet?"

"It was a success." Shane tilted his hat back and grinned. "Had no doubt she'd get it this time."

"This whole embryo-transfer thing fascinates me. In my day, horses did their mating the old-fashioned way. Speaking of which, how is it going between you and Lexi? I noticed you came in very late the other night. Does that mean you two had a good date?"

"I wouldn't call dinner at the Ragin' Cajun with eight other people a date, Mom." Shane had hoped to get a little alone time with Lexi that night, but they were celebrating their friend Aaron's birthday, and while Lexi had agreed to go with him, she made sure they were never truly alone. "I wish she would trust me more instead of always doing this group thing."

"Give her time, honey." Kay placed her hand over her son's heart. "It wasn't that long ago that you were chasing any female with a pulse, and some of them didn't even have that qualification."

"Ouch, Mom." While he loved his mother for always telling him how it was, her words stung. "I haven't been with anyone since the wedding and it's not for a lack of available women."

"Okay, I may love you unconditionally but that doesn't mean I want to hear about your sex life." Kay wrinkled her nose and feigned a shiver. "You keep those bits and your own bits to yourself. Do you hear me?"

"Yes, ma'am." Shane threw his arms around his mother and gave her a hug. Since his father, Joe, died last year of a sudden heart attack, he realized how short life was and how much he took for granted. He swore he wouldn't repeat past mistakes, especially when it came to family. They meant the world to him and someday he hoped to convince Lexi she did, too.

Kay Langtry was the strongest woman Shane knew. His father's will left Shane and his three brothers the business end of the ranch, while the land, houses and the winery were left to their mother. In honor of their father, and after a power struggle that almost tore the family apart, the brothers created an equine facility showcasing the spirit of the horse and the grand opening was next week. Kay ran the Dance of Hope hippotherapy facility and Shane and his brother Chase ran the Ride 'em High! Rodeo School. His brother Cole primarily focused on the Bridle Dance Ranch itself and the breeding programs with Lexi while his other brother Jesse had his own ranch to run.

Once more, his thoughts settled on the mahogany-haired bombshell inside the stables. Every day she was there and every night he tried to shake free the memories of how much he hurt her.

"Aren't you going to be late picking up Hunter?" Kay looked up at her son.

"I'm leaving now." Shane checked his watch. It took an hour and a half to drive to the airport and the flight arrived shortly after. "I love you, Mom."

Giving his mother a peck on the cheek, he hopped into his black, topless and doorless Jeep and removed the keys from the visor. He accidentally popped the clutch and shot off with a cloud of dust in his wake. He'd hear about that one later from his mother. She hated when they spun out of the parking area.

After fighting traffic the entire way to the San Antonio airport, Shane surprisingly found a parking spot close to the entrance. Inside he scanned the incoming board for Hunter's flight.

Flight 3492 11:48 a.m.—On Time

With twenty minutes to spare, he sauntered to the ticket counter and zeroed in on the fresh-faced blonde in a white long-sleeve blouse and dark, fitted vest.

"There's supposed to be a gate pass waiting for me," he drawled. "I'm picking up Hunter Rathbone."

Her brown doe eyes met his and she smiled, a slightly imperfect, yet adorable grin with one tooth barely overlapping the other on the bottom row. Fumbling with the mouse, she inhaled nervously, causing her name tag to glint in the overhead fluorescent lights.

"I can check in to that for you." There was a hint of shyness in her voice and Shane wondered if she was new to the job. Typing in some information on the computer, she asked, "May I see your identification?"

Removing his billfold from his front pocket, he removed his driver's license and slid it across the counter. "Are you new here, Lily?"

When her fingers accidentally grazed his, she hesitated and stared down at his empty ring finger. *Why do women do that?* Tilting his head to catch her gaze, he watched Lily's cheeks turn a deep crimson when she realized she'd been caught doing the typical wedding-ring check. "I started a few weeks ago." Taking another deep breath, she tightened her grip on his license, pulled it toward her and verified his information.

"Do you like it?" Amused by her reaction, Shane decided to have a little fun and leaned on the counter, smiling easily when she swallowed hard and her pupils dilated.

"Yes—here's your gate pass. You'll need to go through security first then head to gate B8." She handed him his license and a map of the airport, trying to avoid any further eye contact.

Shane nodded politely, returned his wallet to his pocket and glanced at the map. "Thanks, darling." He confidently strode away from the counter knowing Lily was probably enjoying the view.

Yep, I still got it. He only wished Lexi thought so, too.

A couple he assumed were embarking on their honeymoon stood ahead of him at the security checkpoint, arms entwined, whispering I-love-you's to each other every few seconds. Shane fought the rude comment that teetered on the tip of his tongue, knowing it came from the hard reminder of what he'd had and lost, and wanted back with only one person.

He turned his attention to the woman in the next aisle who was balancing toddler twin boys in matching overalls on either hip. The strain of the day already evident in her face, and he sincerely hoped she was meeting someone and not heading out on a flight of her own.

He tugged off his boots, placed them on the conveyer belt and emptied his pockets into the bin. After the obligatory pat-down that left him a little uncomfortable, he hopped on one foot while he pulled on his boots.

Exiting the checkpoint at the same time, the frazzled

woman struggled with her children's shoes, reminding Shane how difficult it could be to stuff a kicking foot into a tiny sneaker. Not much more than in her early twenties, she haphazardly tucked a lock of hair, which had escaped her loose ponytail, behind her ear.

"Steven, stay next to Mommy." She kneeled in front of one child, jammed his pudgy foot into the shoe and fastened the Velcro closure while looking over her shoulder at her other restless child. "Steven, come here."

The words were all it took for the child to giggle loudly and take off down the terminal. The woman stood to chase after him, catching her purse strap on the chair.

Shane ran after him, smiling at the boy's duck-waddle steps. For a moment, he felt like he'd time-warped to the days when he thought Dylan was his son. The sudden ache in his heart caught him off guard when he swung the toddler into his arms. The woman quickly caught up with him, frustration creasing her brow.

"Thank you." She reached out for the boy. "I can't believe they made me take their shoes off. Really, thanks again."

Before he responded, the woman went on her way down the terminal.

A few minutes passed once he arrived in the designated waiting area and the gate door opened. A flight attendant emerged with a lanky dark-haired, ice-blue-eyed preteen in tow. Shane approached them and gave Hunter a hug.

"It's good to see you again." Shane released him to get a better look at the soon-to-be man. "You've shot up these past few months."

Shane had met Hunter Rathbone and his parents in Denver during a high school rodeo clinic he'd led in

April. Hunter raved that Shane was his idol, and when Shane mentioned he was opening the Ride 'em High! Rodeo School, Hunter practically begged his parents on the spot to let him attend the school's inaugural session. Shane kept the Rathbones apprised of the school's progress and even flew out to a couple of Hunter's events. He was drawn to the kid's talent and natural ease in the saddle. The fact that Hunter and Dylan were close to the same age caused Shane to wonder more in recent months about the child he'd lost.

Hunter beamed. "I can't believe I'm actually here with you. This is a dream of a lifetime."

"Easy, kid, you have a whole lot of living to do." Shane winked at the attractive flight attendant and handed her his license and gate pass. "Trust me when I say you have much better things to dream of when you get older."

"I wasn't sure if you were picking me up or if someone else from the school was. I'm so excited we're staying in bunkhouses. Just like real cowboys."

"You are a real cowboy." Shane tousled the boy's hair. "Half your class is coming in from out of state. You and one other are flying in, the rest are driving. And since you're our first official student, I thought I should be the one to meet you."

Shane wondered if he'd see Dylan's name on the student manifest one day. An impossible pipe dream considering Tab probably knew more about the rodeo than he did. He hadn't come across Dylan on the circuit yet, but with a bull-riding champion for a father, rodeo coursed through the boy's blood. He'd heard Tab retired, married and had more children after he gained full custody of Dylan. As far as he knew, Dylan had a good life, and in the end, that's what mattered most to Shane.

There were days he wondered if Dylan remembered their time together, and realized it was unlikely. Dylan had just turned a year old when Tab left with him, and after the way Shane had shoved Sharon out the door, he wasn't sure he wanted to be remembered for treating the child's mother that way. Not that she'd win any parent-of-the-year awards. Rumor had it she was down in Brazil trying her hand with another country's cowboys.

"I hope you're ready for a month of hard work?" Shane asked while they rode the escalator down to the baggage claim area.

"Tight!" Hunter said with enthusiasm. "I can't wait to get started."

"Tight?" Shane stopped walking and looked at Hunter's feet. "Are your boots pinching or something?"

"Huh?" Hunter tilted his head and slowly looked from Shane to his feet. "What are you talking about?"

"You said *tight.* What's *tight?*" Shane asked.

Hunter patted Shane on the back and urged him to walk forward before they caused a traffic jam at the bottom of the escalator. "How do I translate this for you, old man? *Tight* means the same as *cool* back in your day. You don't hang with many kids, do you?"

"No, I don't." *Old man?* Shane's ego took a bit of a hit at the comment. "And for the record, thirty-one's not old."

"In terms of a hundred being the oldest, no, you still have time. I'm sure I can teach you enough in the next month to survive the average kid. But since you're practically old enough to be my dad, it may take a little work."

"Oh, nice shot." Shane arm nudged the teen. "We'll see who teaches who this month."

His anticipation of the next four weeks began to shift, nervousness replacing his usual confidence. Maybe teenagers weren't so easy after all.

Chapter Two

"Surprise!"

"Oh, good Lord!" Miranda wobbled backward, her hands protectively on her round belly. "Don't you people know never to startle a pregnant woman?"

"Now I told you to surprise her, not surprise the young'uns out of her." Mable's mocha cheeks flared with a hint of red. "We don't need a repeat of last year, but Tess, honey, ready the shower curtain liner, just in case." Originally, Double Trouble's house manager, Mable became a surrogate mother of sorts when Miranda moved to town and purchased the ranch. Never having had children of her own, Mable doted on Miranda as if she were her own daughter. Since Miranda's drunk of a mother had died a few years ago, Mable easily filled the void in her life.

Lexi doubted anyone would soon forget the day Vicki Slater went into labor shortly after her own baby shower ended. Miranda was right there to catch the bundle of joy in the middle of her living room. So indebted to her friend, Vicki named her daughter Randi Lynn, after Miranda.

Randi Lynn had celebrated her first birthday a few days ago and Miranda had a few weeks before she and

Jesse welcomed twins. Once their honeymoon started, they immediately went to work in the baby-making department. But they weren't the only children with a birthday this time of year. One was missing. Lexi tried to push the thought from her mind.

Lexi had liked Miranda from the day she pulled into town, determined to start a new life. She'd been down that road herself and anyone with the courage to make that kind of move had her vote. Jesse couldn't have chosen a better bride—they were perfectly matched in their fire and passion.

Inside Cole and his wife Tess's newly renovated cottage, Ramblewood's women gathered, showering the latest mommy-to-be with gifts. And Jesse, the only male in the room, seemed to relish the attention. Tess and Cole's adopted daughter, Ever, helped hand Miranda her presents, although Lexi sensed she wanted to tear into each one of them herself.

"I just thought of something," Miranda said, straightening her back to rub it. "I didn't see any cars when we pulled up. Where did you all park?"

Everyone laughed.

"That was an adventure of its own," Mazie, Lexi's younger sister, giggled.

"That son of mine almost lost a few of your guests along the way," Kay said. "We had everyone park at the winery and Shane chauffeured them here in that blasted Jeep of his. Poor Bridgett almost flew out of it."

On a quarter-of-a-million-acre ranch, it was a cinch to hide a few cars. Besides being Dance of Hope's CEO, Kay oversaw the small ranch winery, and since it wasn't open on Saturdays, it was the last place Miranda would venture.

Feeling wistful, Lexi looked around the cottage at the people she considered her extended family. Lexi's parents had grown up with both Tess and Vicki's parents, and then all their kids grew up together. Now a new generation had begun and the cycle would repeat. *Minus one.*

Everyone had been surprised when Shane offered to renovate the house for Cole as a peace offering for trying to block the Dance of Hope hippotherapy facility last year. When Shane and Chase battled Cole and Jesse for control of the ranch's finances, Kay had been relegated to watching her family tear itself apart. Looking around now, Lexi admired the extensive attention to detail Shane had given the remodel.

Recently her friends' lives had changed drastically. They were married and creating families of their own. She'd wanted the same for herself thirteen years ago, if Shane hadn't cheated on her. Lexi tried not to dwell on the what-ifs, but the past still tormented her every day. Especially now that she and Shane were testing the waters again, even though she'd made it clear she wasn't sure where it would lead.

"Honey, did you see Ever's bedroom?"

"Mom…" Lexi shushed her mother. "Are you snooping?"

"No, I'm not snooping," Judy said. "I merely observed the room across the hall when I came out of the bathroom. It's adorable with purple ponies in tiaras painted on the walls. And did you see the mini hitching post out front for Ever's horse? She's one lucky little girl."

Lexi watched the five-year-old across the room. She was sitting on Tess's lap in a lilac party dress, her legs encased in braces up to her knees. Ever had a mild form of cerebral palsy, but physical therapy and daily hippo-therapy sessions had increased her strength and ability to the point where she didn't rely on her crutches much anymore. Surrounded by horses her entire life, Lexi was still in awe of the therapy that utilized the animals' movements to treat people with injuries and physical disabilities.

"She certainly is," Lexi agreed. "Cole told me the day may come when she won't need the braces."

"Isn't Cole such a darling with her?" Judy asked. "All the Langtry men are angels except that Shane. He can't keep it in his pants long enough to—"

"Mom, please." Lexi held up her hand. "Let's not go down this road again. Enjoy the party and stop trying to fight my battles from years ago."

"Who's talking years? I've seen the way you two look at each other. And just the other day, Charlotte Hargrove told me—"

Not wanting to hear any more, Lexi left her mother and walked down the hallway to the bathroom, allowing herself a glance in Ever's room. Cutely decorated with its feminine frills, she remembered the animated way Shane had described the low wall-length banquette he'd built under the window so Ever could easily sit on it without assistance.

Inside the bathroom, she locked the door and rested against it. Light cornflower-blue paint decorated the upper half of the wall over white wainscoting. A tiny walker stood near the white pedestal sink. Grip bars of various heights lined the wall next to the tub so she could lift herself out without relying on someone to help her. Shane had thought of everything.

She had to hand it to him. And in his care for his

little niece, Lexi knew Shane still missed Dylan, even though he refused to speak his name.

The walls suddenly seemed to close in on Lexi. Her chest tightened and she desperately needed the freedom of wide open spaces, preferably on the back of a horse. Ducking out the kitchen door, she walked to the side of the house, safely out of view.

Lexi slid to the ground and closed her eyes. Flashes from that Colorado hospital room flooded her vision and she wrapped her arms around herself. This time of year was the hardest and memories she'd rather forget invaded almost every thought.

"Lexi?" a voice called to her. "Are you all right?"

Her head shot up. Silhouetted against the sun, Shane sat astride Ransom. Shielding the light from her eyes, Lexi wasn't able to see the other riders, but she quickly made out Dream Catcher's unusual silver dappled legs and assumed their friend Clay Tanner was astride the horse. Considering the other horses she saw were under her care, the riders must be students.

"I'm fine," she said. "I pulled a muscle earlier and it's acting up—hardly worth mentioning. What are you doing here? I thought you'd want to be miles away from a house full of women and baby talk."

"Shane finally let us out of the classroom," one of the young students called out while the rest of them laughed.

Shane maneuvered his mount away from Lexi. "You'll be in the arena tomorrow. I warned you this wasn't all fun and games." Nudging the horse forward with his legs he nodded at Lexi. "Are you sure you're okay? You look awfully pale."

"Thank you, but I'm good," Lexi choked out. She

wanted to forget the past and find some happiness in her life.

"See you later," the students called out.

Lexi waved, closed her eyes and wondered if her son had the rodeo bug...wherever he was.

"Who was that?" Hunter rode up alongside Shane.

"That was trouble with a capital *T*," Shane grumbled. "Let me give you some advice, kid. Don't get married."

"You and Trouble were married?" Hunter asked. "Wow, she's pretty."

"No, Trouble and I weren't married," Shane said. "And her name's Lexi. We could have been, though, if I hadn't screwed things up."

"What'd you do?"

"*I* got married." Shane looked over his shoulder. "The trail narrows up ahead when we get closer to the stream. Let the horse do the work, they know these trails."

Shane nudged his horse ahead of Hunter, ending the conversation. He didn't want to remember what he'd lost with Lexi. The pain he'd caused reflected in her eyes whenever she looked at him, and the guilt he carried for breaking her heart was always present.

Lexi had remained close to his family, and he'd managed a friendship with her, but for the longest time, he'd vowed never to be alone with her. He didn't think either one of their hearts could take it. But once things began to change between them in recent months, Shane had allowed himself to dream of the day she'd let her guard down enough to spend time alone with him, secretly vowing to make things right between them.

At the top of his game now, Shane had a school to run with Chase and a full schedule of rodeos to ride in.

The world all-around title eluded him so far and he was determined to win it before Chase did. With the help of Jesse and Cole, who filled in when needed, along with the rest of their teaching staff, he and Chase still actively competed in the rodeo and against each other. Friendly in their competition, the boys were in a tight race to bring home the grand prize. Shane wanted that championship more than anything…well, almost.

Since they'd broken ground on the new facility, Shane had found himself in Lexi's vicinity more often than not. It was all he could do to prevent her from distracting him in his quest to win that coveted belt buckle. Being able to say Ride 'em High! was owned by a world all-around champion would help make the school the best in the country. Their facility offered everything from rodeo clown bullfighting and rough-stock training to barrel racing and roping, and Shane wanted his students to walk away with the confidence and knowledge it took to best any competitor they came across. What better way to do that than with a champion as your instructor?

"How about a drink at Slater's Mill later?" Shane asked his best friend, Clay Tanner, when they arrived back at the stables. "I need some adult time, if you know what I mean."

"All right." Clay removed his saddle. "You need help returning the women to their cars?"

"Nope, Chase has those honors." Shane removed his straw Stetson and wiped his brow with the back of his arm. The last day of June meant it was the start of the sweltering season. They'd designed the new facility with an indoor arena, and divided it in half. Hippotherapy had one side of the building and the rodeo school had the other. It would allow horse and rider to work without the Texas sun exhausting them. But at Kay's insistence, until the official ribbon-cutting next week, instructors and students had to ride outside. Classes would be taught at the picnic tables near the main corral.

A few hours later, Shane made his way back to the main house for a shower and a change of clothes. After double-checking that Chase was staying in as the bunkhouse den dad for the night, Shane headed out for a kid-free evening. Slater's Mill usual Saturday night crowd gathered near the bar. Different ball games played on the screens while Elvis Watts and his band belted out a cover of "Red Solo Cup." Lifting a longneck to his mouth, he stopped midswig when he noticed a familiar sexy number shake and shimmy on the dance floor in turquoise boots and jeans so tight they must have been painted on.

Making his way through the crowd, he two-stepped next to her. "Hey, sugar britches, how's that pulled muscle?"

Lexi swung to face him, not losing rhythm with the music. "It was a polite way of saying none of your business, Shane. Don't take it personally."

Before he responded, she danced her way to the edge of the floor and dropped into the circular booth where the regulars congregated. The roster had changed over the past year. Shane's cousin Brandon and his wife Vicki had a little one to tend to at home, but Brandon still popped in from time to time to help bartend for his dad, Charlie, who owned the honky-tonk. Since adopting Ever, Cole and Tess stayed home most nights. Jesse and Miranda had two of their own on the way. The crowd had dwindled down to Bridgett, a waitress in town, Lexi,

Clay and Chase. Shane wondered which of them would be the next to jump ship. At this rate, he was willing to bet he'd be the last one standing.

Placing his empty on the bar, he looked down the row of men, most sitting by themselves. Men once like him, now past their prime and alone. Was this his future? A lonely old man at a bar, night after night?

Kendra Anderson, Lexi's cousin, slipped in next to him and handed Charlie her orders.

"When do you go on break?" Shane asked the well-rounded waitress.

"In about twenty minutes." Her red tank top strained and dipped in the right places, leaving little to the imagination. "Let me guess, you're going to drill me about Lexi again?"

"I need your advice—" Shane halted at her laughter.

"Either marry her or forget her, but stop flounder-flopping about it already."

"We have a special guest singer tonight," Elvis boomed from the stage. "Let's give a big round of applause for our hometown girl, Lexi Lawson."

Lexi slinked across the stage with her arms in the air, rousing the crowd. She turned her back to the audience and picked up a vintage red Fender Telecaster, tuning it to her satisfaction. When she played a twangy, steady beat, the crowd roared, recognizing the tune. Facing her audience, she strode to the microphone, owning the stage. Looking right at him, she began singing Taylor Swift's "I Knew You Were Trouble."

Mesmerized for a moment, he felt like they were alone and she was singing only to him, even if it wasn't the nicest of songs. Breaking her gaze, Shane threw a ten on the bar and headed for the door. Her voice was as intoxicating as she was beautiful, and if he stayed a second longer, he'd wind up making a fool of himself in front of the entire town.

THE CROWD SCREAMING at her feet and the blinding lights didn't block out the sight of Shane leaving. Opening a bottle of water that Bridgett handed her from the side of the stage, Lexi knew she'd probably upset Shane when she directed the song to him. Over the past few years she had watched the man drift from one woman to the next while he never cared how hard it was on her. Lexi still wasn't sure how much he'd legitimately changed, but she had noticed he wasn't catting around like he used to.

A part of her saw the old Shane she'd fallen in love with start to reemerge, but despite his newfound loyalty to her, she also knew the man had tunnel vision when it came to winning the championship. Admittedly, Lexi wasn't sure what kind of life she'd be able to build with Shane when she was a little jealous of the dream he chased. Truth was, she blamed their demise on the rodeo.

The band invited her to sing a few more songs, and when she finally stepped off the stage with an adrenaline rush and smile of satisfaction, she searched the bar, but Shane still wasn't anywhere in sight. Not that it mattered. She was perfectly capable of having a nice evening out without Shane Langtry. She'd been doing it for years, but if she was honest with herself, she'd concede that she did enjoy having him around.

Bridgett leaned into her once she was back in the booth. "I assure you he left empty-handed tonight."

"Bridge, I'm not his keeper." Lexi pulled her hair up and off her shoulders. "He's a free man."

"Oh, please, Shane hasn't been a free man since you two broke up after high school. Someday you two will get a clue," Bridgett said.

Kendra set a folded note and two beers on the table and popped the tops off. "Compliments of the man in the tan shirt at the bar."

The three women turned to look at the stranger. He lifted a hand to wave and tipped his hat as Lexi read his scribble.

"Did you read this?" Lexi asked.

Kendra shook her head.

Lexi's eyes narrowed as she rose from the booth, grabbed both bottles and honed in on the man.

"Oh, dear, what's she going to do?" Kendra asked. "Charlie's going to be ticked off at whatever it is."

"This isn't going to be good," Bridgett replied. "I'll settle our tab because I have a feeling this night is about to end."

Weaving in and out of the crowd, Lexi approached the tawny-haired, middle-aged man with a mustache in dire need of a trim. She lifted her hands in front of her, the longnecks dangling from her fingers.

"Did you send these to my table?"

He winked. "I sure did."

"So you thought it was appropriate to ask—how was it you put it?" Lexi unfolded the note and read it aloud. "For a *redhead-and-brunette sandwich?* Honestly, if that's the extent of your creativity, I think we'd be incredibly bored."

"I, uh, I can teach you a few things." The man leered at her chest, making his greasy hair all the more obvious.

"Really? I can teach you a few things, too." Lexi winked in return.

"I bet you can." He openly gave her body a once-over while making a disgusting clicking noise with his tongue. "Where do we start?"

"Lesson one." Lexi held the beers above his crotch and poured out the contents, then slammed the bottles down on the bar. "Asking a woman and her friend for a threesome is just plain rude."

"Dammit, Lexi!" Charlie yelled from behind the bar. "Stop pouring drinks on my customers."

"Sorry, Charlie." Lexi laughed and headed toward the door.

SHANE SAT IN his Jeep and listened to Lexi sing. Standing and staring at her in the middle of a crowded bar sure didn't do his heart any favors. No, it was safer outside where he wouldn't be tempted to rush the stage and kiss her in front of the entire town.

Lexi and Bridgett burst through Slater's double doors laughing hysterically. Unnoticed, he watched them as they walked by. The two women climbed into Lexi's black Mustang convertible and drove off, their laughter carrying across the parking lot. A man thundered out of the bar behind them, swearing at their car.

Shane ventured a guess at what had happened from the way the man wiped at his jeans. It wasn't the first time Lexi dumped a drink on someone. He wondered what the poor sap had done to warrant such a response. She had a fiery temper when it came to men and he felt he was to blame for her defensive attitude. The country girl who left for college never returned. In her place was an extremely independent woman with walls so high, no one could possibly scale them—but he would damn sure try.

"What are you doing out here? I thought we were getting a drink." Clay braced his arms on the roll bar above the Jeep's passenger seat. "I saw Lexi and Bridgett peel out of here. You look unscathed, so who was her victim?"

"Some guy." Shane shrugged. "Listen, I'm not up for another round in there tonight. Care to grab something at the Still 'n' Grill instead?"

"When are you going to admit you've never gotten over her?" Clay laughed when Shane tried to take a swing at him. "Hey, I just call 'em as I see 'em. You've had two loves in your life. Lexi and the rodeo. Swallow your pride and tell her, because you've exhausted the entire female population in town. Literally and figuratively."

"Okay, Mr. P.I." Having a private investigator for a best friend made keeping a secret next to impossible. "Here's a fact for you—she's not in love with me."

"Really? Because from where I stand, she never stopped loving you." Clay looked across the parking lot toward Shelby Street. "Why don't you go after her and end this insanity? My God, you've been celibate for how many months now and don't tell me it's because you suddenly have the urge to wait until marriage."

"I've been busy building the school."

"You've been busy pining over Lexi," Clay flatly stated. "I'm not the only one who's noticed. Just about all of Ramblewood was at Jesse and Miranda's wedding and we all saw the look on both of your faces when you escorted Lexi down that aisle."

"What do you want me do?" Shane threw his hands in the air. "Knock on her door and say, 'Hey, Lex, I love you, let's get married'? She'd annihilate me and you know it."

"This isn't an eight-second ride, Shane." Clay laughed. "You don't have to charge the woman like a bull out of the chute. But you could up the ante and do something special for her."

"Like what?" The thought of surprising Lexi piqued Shane's interest.

"You know her better than I do. You'll come up with an idea." Clay playfully punched Shane in the arm. "Come on, let's head to the Still 'n' Grill and we'll try to come up with a plan over a beer."

Shane doubted one or two surprises would convince Lexi to trust him again, but he'd do almost anything if it meant winning her heart.

Chapter Three

"First day of groundwork, men. I know it's early but we have a lot to cover today before the ribbon cutting." Shane led his fifteen students from the bunkhouse after a predawn workout and hearty breakfast they'd prepared together. "Some of you are more experienced than others and some of you don't have any experience. That's all right. There's no ride limit, but I don't want you to push yourself to the point of injury, either."

"These are our saddle broncs," Chase explained, taking over from Shane. "They're larger than our barebacks. I want to reiterate to everyone that we have zero tolerance for animal abuse. If we even suspect it, you are out of here. We do not condone or authorize the use of cattle prods or sharpened spurs in any rough-stock event. Before you enter any chute here on the ranch, your rowels will be checked, so if they're sharp, get them off."

When Shane and Chase designed the monthlong intensive rodeo class, they did it with serious competitors in mind. They offered two monthlong sessions for junior-rodeo children in the summer and more personalized programs for people of all ages the remainder of the year.

Stressing safety first, Ride 'em High! was one of the

few schools in the country with a weeklong classroom schedule. They decided to include a grueling conditioning program to ensure the students were in top physical condition. At the ranch's small fitness center, a trainer met with the students every day and put them through rodeo boot camp to build their core muscles. When the kids left for home, the trainers recommended they join a local fitness center to maintain their strength and flexibility.

"Most of our competition broncs are six to seven years old," Shane continued. "The ones we're using today are older and not as feisty. We don't make these horses buck. It's a natural instinct and they're bred to buck. A good portion of the horses you see in competition are there because no one could ride them. Some were untrainable, others are rescues.

"Hunter, you're up." Shane waved the boy to the front. "We're starting off this morning with some saddle work."

Shane proceeded to explain the difference between saddle bronc and bareback rigging, then introduced the local college kids, home for the summer, who had volunteered to check riggings and help the students.

A saddle had been set on a large barrel attached to a wide base for training purposes. Hunter climbed on and set his boots high in the stirrups. With pointed toes, he rocked his hips slightly and squared his shoulders with the saddle. He gripped the thick braided rein and held it out over the center of the saddle swells, his other hand up in the air as if he were swearing on a stack of bibles.

"Tuck your chin a little." Shane pointed to the hole between the swells and the seat. "Look here the entire time. Visualize setting your spurs above the horse's shoulders. Raise your legs and tighten your abs."

Shane ran through the steps of riding a saddle bronc, amazed at the ease Hunter exhibited in every movement. Many of the kids reminded Shane of himself at that age. Determined, confident and willing to do anything to fulfill their dreams of turning pro. He couldn't help but wonder if this was how it would have felt training Dylan.

"My abs are about to give out!" Hunter yelled through his last mock ride.

"You're working your core." Shane placed a hand on his shoulder to still him. "This is why we're working you so hard on the stabilizing platform and the vertical leg raises. A weak core will get you thrown. Great job, Hunter. Who's next?"

"This is one of the toughest events to master," Chase said. "But I promise you, after this workout you will feel muscles you didn't think you had and you'll thank us for it."

Everyone took their turn, including Chase, who admitted he liked the barrel for an alternative abdominal workout.

"You must synchronize every moment with the horse in order to get the most fluid ride possible." Shane shrugged on his own vest. "And if you don't mark your ride, you won't receive a score. To mark, your heels must touch the horse's shoulders at the first jump from the chute."

Shane hopped the fence and made his way to the chute, where a horse waited. Measuring his hack rein over the back of the horse, he grabbed hold of the thick braided rope and slid into the saddle, placing his feet all the way into the stirrups. Lifting up his rein hand, he nodded and the gate opened.

On the saddle bronc, in the middle of the arena, was the only place he could completely forget about the past and concentrate on the moment.

LEXI AWOKE BEFORE the first rooster crowed. You wouldn't find anyone sleeping in at the Lawsons' house. Sixth-generation farmers, they were champing at the bit to start their day long before the sun came up. Lexi's younger brother, Nash, maintained the petting zoo animals while their father, uncle and cousins tended the fields. Her mother and aunt ran the market and gift store.

Situated right off the interstate, the 130-acre farm dated back to 1820. The original barn had been converted into a retail market and gourmet kitchen in the early fifties, catering to tourists as they drove through the state. Lexi's sister Mazie learned to cook in that kitchen, leading her to open the Bed & Biscuit in the center of town.

The Lawsons gave visitors the true farm experience, from the petting zoo to fresh picked produce, some of which the customers were allowed to harvest themselves. Strawberry and pumpkin season filled the fields with people, but the two-acre corn maze around Halloween drew the biggest crowds.

The horses were Lexi's domain. Before showering, she headed down to the barn and fed the family's handful of horses. Once she checked her schedule for the day, she saddled Autumn's Secret and surveyed the property. Their morning and evening routine allowed Lexi to escape from the rest of the world.

Robert Smith Surtees wrote, "There is no secret so

close as that between a rider and his horse." The quote had inspired the name of her mare, which she helped foal on the Langtrys' farm the first fall she returned from Cornell. Seeing how much Lexi was enamored with the horse, Joe Langtry bestowed the mare upon her—a little assurance she'd stay in town. She trained Autumn herself, and while man's best friend worked for some, horses bore Lexi's secrets, and she was confident they wouldn't be shared.

Lexi swung by the Magpie for a cup of coffee since she had to wait for the Critter Care animal hospital to open its doors. Shorted on tetanus vaccines in yesterday's shipment, she needed to borrow a few doses for the pregnant mares due to foal in the next six weeks. Lexi had had more problems of late with her supplier and needed Ashleigh to research a new one before the week's end.

"I have a bone to pick with you," Charlie Slater said from the corner table.

"Take a number," Lexi replied while Bridgett waited for her to order, doing little to keep a straight face. "If Maggie's made any banana nut muffins today, I'll have one of those and a large coffee, extra hot in case I have to pour it on some unsuspecting patron."

"If you're going to chase my customers off, you can't come around the Mill anymore." Charlie never referred to his own last name when talking about his bar.

"Bridge, make mine to go." Pulling a few bills out of her pocket, she handed them to her friend. "I'll cover Charlie's breakfast to make up for the one, possibly two, beers that rude boy might've ordered. Oh, wait, that's right, he did order them—and wore them."

"If you don't tell Charlie what that guy wanted the

other night, I will." Bridgett gave Lexi her change. "You were justified."

"I don't want you buying my breakfast." Charlie swiveled to face her. "I want you to stop assaulting people. One of these days, you're going to start a riot. That man was furious."

"Let him think what he wants." Lexi shrugged. "I'm sure there was a time or two that I dumped a drink on someone for lesser reasons. Let it go."

"If you say so." Bridgett placed a muffin in a white paper bag and handed Lexi her order. "I'll catch up with you at the ribbon cutting this afternoon."

Lexi stopped by Charlie's table on her way out. "People bought more drinks when I got on that stage than they did all night with Elvis playing the same drivel he plays every Saturday. I did you a favor, so the way I see it, we're even. Trust me when I say, you don't want his kind around there."

A few minutes later Lexi pulled into the animal hospital's parking lot. She knew Mazie probably saw her from the kitchen window of the Bed & Biscuit next door and would want to talk. When the old Victorian went up for sale a few years ago, Mazie realized its proximity to the animal hospital and the bark park would attract future clients by catering to their pets' every need.

Checking her watch, Lexi knew fifteen minutes wasn't enough time to visit with her sister. She loved Mazie, but her propensity to chat for hours wore thin when Lexi had a packed day ahead of her. Relieved when she saw Dr. Cerf park his SUV, she quickly picked up the vaccines and headed to Bridle Dance.

Lexi's cell phone rang.

"Good morning, Mazie," Lexi said without even looking at the caller ID.

"You should have stopped in. I'm pulling one of your favorites out of the oven right now. Spinach and mushroom frittata. Do you have time to turn around and have a little breakfast? We haven't had a chance to really talk in a few weeks."

"I'm sorry, my schedule is super tight today." Lexi turned off the main road. "I have a lot to do before the ribbon cutting, but I promise we'll catch up there. I love you, sis, but right now, I do have to go."

Lexi dropped the phone on the seat next to her and rolled her shoulders to ease the stress she felt starting to build. She loved her job, but some days, the constant running between ranches wore thin.

The rearing bronze horse statues at the entrance to Bridle Dance glinted in the morning light. The fully expanded foliage of the pecan trees shaded the entire length of the dirt road, while puddles of water formed near their trunks from the ranch's buried drip irrigation. Lexi's father had helped Joe Langtry design the system to maintain constant water levels during the summer dry spells.

A white canopy stood off to the side of the new equine facility in preparation for the afternoon ceremony. The massive building with beige siding sat behind a series of corrals used for the rodeo school. The rear of the building incorporated secluded pastures for hippotherapy use. In front of the double carriage-house-inspired entrance, two statues were draped in dark cloth and tied at the bottom, waiting for their unveiling in a few hours.

Local cowboys gathered around the nearest round

pen. "When are you going to marry me, Lexi?" one of them called out to her.

"When you're old enough to shave," she hollered back.

"I'm twenty-one. I'm legal." The other men egged him on. "You don't know what you're missing."

"You boys go on." Nicolino waved them off. "Good morning, Lexi. Will you be at the grand opening today? Ella was talking about you this morning, saying how long it's been since she's seen you."

Shouts came from within one of the corrals. With a quick nod in her direction, Shane sat atop a bareback and raised his arm in the air to signal the chute gate to open. Bucking wildly, man and horse twisted and turned through the dust-filled eight-second ride. With all the flair and skill he'd exhibit in a competitive event, Shane grabbed his pickup man as he rode by and dismounted with the grace of a gymnast, bowing her way.

Lexi shook her head and redirected her attention to Nicolino. Starting out as a ranch hand fresh from Italy when Lexi was in grade school, the newcomer had barely spoken a word of English when Joe hired him. He'd grown to be a part of their family and married Kay's niece Ella Slater, the eldest daughter of her brother Charlie. Five kids and two loyal decades later, Cole had promoted him to general operations manager in January. Raised in the *butteri* cowboy tradition, he opted to wear heavy cotton pants and a wide-brimmed hat instead of chaps and a Stetson. The mazzarella staff he carried was used to threaten unruly teenagers more than it was to herd the horses.

"I'll be there." Lexi looked in the stalls. "I have a

couple of mares to vaccinate and some paperwork to fill out here, then I'll return after making my rounds."

"Don't you want to stick around and see the show Shane's putting on for you?" Nicolino feigned shock that she'd dare leave in the middle of such an event.

"Eh, you've seen one, you've seen them all."

Nicolino's laughter followed her through the open doors.

Rivaling the size of a football field, the country French stone-and-stucco facility featured Craftsman-style windows and timber archways. A ground-level covered walkway with exposed rafters encircled the building. A large second-story cupola was perched atop the center of the sand-colored structure and housed the ranch's main office, while miniature cupolas lined the roof on either side, allowing extra light to filter through to the stalls below.

Joe Langtry had called the building his horse mansion. A better description didn't exist in Lexi's mind. Grooms and trainers hurried about, placing the finishing touches on everything before today's events.

Lexi made her way down the exposed timber interior hallway. Horse stalls with full-height mahogany-stained doors and bars prevented cribbing or chewing. Otherwise the horses could gnaw on the wood and wear down their teeth or cause colic and stomach ulcers.

Not wanting to waste time today with so much to do, she plucked her phone from her pocket and called Billy. "Vaccination lesson today. Meet me in the office so I can show you the forms and then we'll check on Crystal."

Crystal was carrying Joe Langtry's dream baby. Dam Tenny Bay and sire King's Obsession were two of the highest earners in cutting horse competition. Bridle

Dance didn't own either horse, but Joe had arranged the match before his death last year. Determined to see the surrogacy all the way through, the Langtry family had continued with Joe's plans and were anxiously anticipating the foal's arrival. It was the very last project Joe set in motion, and eleven months later, the day was almost upon them.

A few hours later, Lexi gathered her bags and headed outside the stables. She loved a day without problems, especially when she finished ahead of schedule. She swung by the rodeo school and saw Kay Langtry resting her arms on the top rail of the round pen.

"You got it!" Kay shouted to one of the teens astride a bucking horse. "You boys look great out there."

Shane stood outside the pen, Ever perched on a bale of hay next to him. "Ride 'em high like Uncle Shane!" the little girl shouted. Shane lifted her onto his shoulders, giving her a high ride of her own.

"He's really good with her and the rest of the hippotherapy kids," Kay commented, her mood pensive. "How different everything was a year ago."

Lexi draped her arm across the older woman's shoulders and rested her head against Kay's. Joe's heart attack shocked the entire community and the family infighting that ensued for months afterward had taken its toll on the Langtry matriarch, but Kay stuck with her husband's wishes and built the nonprofit hippotherapy facility. Joe wanted a place where anyone who needed help could get it, paying only what they could afford. Converted bunkhouses accommodated families from out of town during long-term therapy. After a battle with Shane and Chase that would have torn most families apart forever, everything finally came to fruition.

"I can't tell you how glad I'll be when this day is over," Kay confessed. "I know it sounds strange, but honestly, once that ribbon is cut on the front door, I'll feel like this family will finally be at peace."

A gangly boy approached Shane and handed Ever a bottle of water. Lifting her from his shoulder, Shane returned the little girl to her hay bale alongside some of the other hippotherapy kids while he watched the students and joined the boy at the rail.

Lexi smiled at his inherent teaching instincts. "I don't think I've seen Shane this content before."

"That Hunter Rathbone sure does dote on him." Kay nodded in the direction of the boy next to Shane. "I can't believe how much he acts like Shane at that age."

Hunter stood on the second rail and waved his hat in the air to cheer on his classmate. His features no longer shadowed, Lexi saw a mop of dark brown hair, ice-blue eyes and a strong angular jaw with the hint of a cleft chin. She felt her stomach turn ever so slightly at the remarkable resemblance to Shane.

Lexi white-knuckled her grip on her satchel. "Where—where is he from?"

"Colorado," Kay replied. "Shane calls him his *Mini-Me*."

The ground beneath Lexi all but disappeared. Squatting down on the grass next to the pen, she feigned fumbling through her bag. Confident she'd regained her footing, she stood and tried to cover her bewilderment. "I must have left my camera in the truck. I—I thought the school would draw mostly a local crowd."

"Next door or the next continent, I think Hunter would follow Shane wherever he taught," Kay continued. "You should hear the child prattle on how Shane's his hero. When Hunter heard about the school, he begged his parents to send him here. Good heavens, are you all right?"

"It must be the heat." Lexi's knees betrayed her and she found herself back on the ground. "I just need a cold shower and I'll be fine."

The events vividly replayed in her mind. Years ago, in late October, Shane surprised Lexi and whisked her away for a romantic weekend at the Devil's Thumb Ranch Resort, a stone's throw from her college campus. They didn't emerge from the cabin until Monday morning, and she barely made it to her first class. Perfect in every way imaginable, their getaway reassured Lexi that they could maintain their relationship while she continued school.

A few weeks later, when Lexi discovered she was pregnant, she rationalized that it had happened for a reason. Planning to have a family one day, Lexi wasn't sure she wanted one now. When her doctor confirmed a July due date, she put faith in perfect timing. She'd be able to continue with college in the fall without missing any classes. Not wanting to discuss it with Shane over the phone, she decided to wait and tell him in person, during winter break. Only he had a surprise of his own.

Devastated by his infidelity, Lexi was scandalized by his quick decision to marry Sharon Vincent, so she immediately returned to school. Clearly showing by spring break, Lexi lied to her family and said she'd enrolled in an internship to avoid coming home. She hated the deception, but after hearing how happy Shane was with his son, Lexi didn't want to ruin his new family. The entire town knew he didn't have an ounce of love for Sharon but Shane tolerated her for Dylan's sake and Lexi resolved that someday he'd learn to love his wife.

Determined to move forward with her career, Lexi painfully gave her baby up for adoption immediately following his birth, believing he'd have a better life with a strong, stable family. It was the hardest thing she'd ever had to do. A mother should never have to give up her child, but it was a sacrifice she willingly made for her son's future.

Not wanting to wonder if every child she saw on the street was hers, Lexi transferred to New York's Cornell University.

A day hadn't passed when she didn't think of him, but she refused to doubt her decision. When she found out Dylan wasn't Shane's, the realization that they could have been a family if he hadn't cheated on her drove her to pieces some nights.

On her visits home, she avoided him at all costs, fearing he would know what she'd done. No one questioned her attitude, since his betrayal was public knowledge, but the guilt she felt whenever someone told her how shattered Shane was and how much he'd changed from a family man, to being wild and reckless since Tab took Dylan away, almost killed her.

Not allowing herself another glance at the boy again, Lexi took Kay's outstretched hand and managed to stand. *This can't be happening.*

"SOMETHING'S WRONG WITH Lexi." Shane started to walk toward his mother and Nicolino as they escorted Lexi to her car. "Ever, stay right there and don't go near the rails. Hunter, will you watch her for a minute?"

"Come on, bro." Chase beckoned to him from the arena. "Let's show them how it's done."

"In a minute." Shane headed in Lexi's direction until he heard her car start and saw Nicolino pat her trunk, seemingly unconcerned as she drove out of the parking area.

A few hours in this heat was enough to wear anyone out and Shane reasoned Lexi had probably overdone it, rushing around trying to be Wonder Woman. The rising temperatures were getting to all of them and Shane decided to end class early so the kids could go down to the river for a swim and cool off before they demonstrated some of their techniques for the crowd later.

Opting to stay behind, Shane had successfully avoided spending any length of time around children since he lost Dylan. One- or two-day rodeo clinics meant attachments were impossible. When Cole and Tess adopted Ever, he became an instant uncle to a precocious four-year-old. By her fifth birthday in April she'd grown to be such a part of his life, he actually sought her out every day. It pained him to think he'd once stood in the way of her progress at the ranch. In eight months, her ability to walk doubled. And with a hippotherapy facility in her own backyard, she didn't have to travel the three hours to therapy anymore.

Once Shane saw the children and adults come to Dance of Hope for therapy evaluation before the grand opening, he finally understood why this project was so dear to his father. It might be too late to apologize for trying to block the facility from being built, but it didn't mean he couldn't do everything in his power to make his family proud of him. He not only wanted their approval, but he also wanted Lexi's.

With all the children on the ranch, thoughts of Dylan had hit him harder than they had in a decade. Shane wondered if the teen ever sat in the stands during his rodeo events. There were times he caught himself checking the rider roster for Tab's name even though Shane knew he'd long since retired.

Plodding toward the small stand-alone office behind the main stables, Shane entered the air-conditioned building. A built-in table wrapped around the entire room and the computers were connected to the main office inside the barn, saving people from traipsing across the courtyard. Shane logged on to the system and opened the web browser.

Cole dropped paperwork into the inbox on the wall as he entered the office. "I'm surprised you didn't go with everyone else down to the river."

"Nah." Shane typed *Dylan Fanning* into the search engine. "I have some things to finish up."

"Don't do it, Shane." Cole stood behind him, staring down at the words on the screen. "Leave it in the past. You know he has a good life with Tab. Why are you dredging this up now?"

Because all these kids remind me of what might have been.

"Note to self, buy a laptop so I can have some privacy." If he knew more about Dylan, he'd have some peace and closure. Anything was better than not knowing. At the very least Shane wanted to find out if he was riding in any of the junior rodeos.

"For the little you use the internet, I'd go with an iPad," Cole said.

"You know you sound just like Dad?" Shane glanced

up at his brother, wishing Cole would leave him alone. This wasn't a moment he wanted to share with anyone.

"Dad would have told you to look it up on your phone. It's capable of doing the same thing."

Shane continued to stare at his brother incredulously. Turning back toward the screen, he let his finger hover above the enter key. Shane swore silently, knowing his brother was right. He pressed and held the delete key until all the letters in Dylan's name disappeared. Annoyed with himself, he stormed from the office and went to check on Siempre, one of their newborn foals. Animals loved you unconditionally, no matter how much of an ass you made of yourself.

LATER THAT AFTERNOON Mayor Darren Fox stood before a microphone in front of the equine facility, Kay by his side. "Thank you for joining us today for this momentous event. I am pleased to introduce Kay Langtry, CEO of Dance of Hope."

Applause spread throughout the ranch when Kay took her place at the microphone, the townsfolk gathered before her.

"Thank you." Pulling a tissue from her pocket, Kay looked into the crowd. "Dance of Hope was my husband's dream. A year ago, I stood by Joe's side when he started designing this facility. And though he's not with us today, I know he's up there watching.

"No amount of words can describe my gratitude to everyone who's participated in this venture. Cole, Jesse, Shane and Chase. My four boys carried out their father's dream, adding the Ride 'em High! Rodeo School to the original plans. Your father would have been so proud of you, as I am today. I love you with all my heart."

The Langtry brothers surrounded Kay, linking their arms in a protective circle around their mother.

Shane looked skyward. "I love you, Dad. This is for you."

Each brother made a brief speech of his own, splitting off to stand beside the covered statues on either side of the facility's entrance.

Jesse and Cole tugged on the cloth, revealing a life-size bronze statue of Ever atop Paco, her hippotherapy horse, with Joe by her side.

"To say our father was smitten with my daughter is an understatement," Cole said. "She inspired him to help others and I'm grateful she had the opportunity to know her grandfather." Holding up an enlarged framed copy of the inspiration photograph for the statue, Cole continued.

"My mother took this the first time dad met Ever. The photo sat on his desk and a day didn't go by that he didn't look at it. Together, we can look upon his memory as he saw it."

Shane and Chase pulled away another cloth, uncovering a bucking horse with a younger version of Joe in the saddle, one arm in the air.

"Our father was a rancher by blood," Shane said, "but a true rodeo cowboy at heart. Back in his day, he outrode the best of them and taught all of us and many of you how to get in that saddle and stay in it." Holding up a photograph, he said, "This is our father's last competitive ride. He held on for eight seconds then walked away from the sport. The next day Cole was born and the tradition was handed down to his children."

The boys joined their mother at the entrance to the

facility, the five of them reaching up to unveil the sign above the carriage house doors:

Dance of Hope & Ride 'em High!
In memory of Joseph Langtry

Lifting the oversize silver scissors, Kay cut the white ribbon spanning the facility's doors. The crowd applauded when the doors swung wide. Leading the way, Kay walked into the stone entryway that divided the two companies and hung both photographs on the awaiting wall hooks.

She turned and opened her arms to the crowd. "Welcome, Ramblewood!"

After the facility tours, the waitstaff bustled in and out of the tent while people milled about the property. Shane swore he shook hands with more people this afternoon than in his entire life.

"You had a great dad," Hunter said beside him. "I think I would have liked him."

"He'd have liked you, too." Shane ruffled the boy's hair. "Let's get something to eat."

Shane had spotted Lexi in the crowd throughout the afternoon, glad to see she felt up to attending the ceremony. Usually composed and in control, she seemed a bit harried and hung near his immediate vicinity, yet still managed to keep her distance. He resisted the urge to check on her, as he was busy with the media. The *Ramblewood Gazette* took photographs while Nola West interviewed Chase for KWTT's evening news.

"Allow me to introduce myself." A man held out his hand to Shane. "I'm Ryan Hammershimer, from Keeping it Reel Pictures, and we'd like to build a reality show around you and your rodeo school."

Shane laughed. "You want to give me a television show?" Wait until his brothers heard about this.

"WHAT ARE YOU doing?" Mazie peered over Lexi's shoulder. "Are you taking pictures of that kid?"

"What kid?" Startled, Lexi quickly saved the photo of Hunter to her phone. "I—I'm trying to get a shot of those statues. They're truly a work of art. I can't believe they were commissioned this quickly."

"What are you hiding?" Mazie insisted. "That was no picture of a statue. What's up?"

"I'm not hiding anything, and even if I were, why would I tell you?" Lexi snapped.

"Well, thanks a lot." Mazie turned her back on Lexi and started to walk away.

"I'm sorry Mazie, I didn't mean that." Lexi caught up to her sister and grabbed her arm. "I have a foal on my mind. I truly am sorry."

"You need a vacation, sis," Mazie said. "You can't worry about work all the time."

"This coming from someone who eats, sleeps and breathes the Bed & Biscuit."

"That's different and you know it. I happen to live there. You don't live in a stable." She turned to leave. "I'm going to get you something to eat, you look like you need some sustenance."

Angling away from her sister, Lexi tried to move closer to Hunter without him noticing. When he laughed, her breath caught in her throat. *He has my laugh.* A mother dreamed of the day she heard her child's laughter for the first time. Today she heard hers.

Lexi watched Shane and Hunter pose for a series of photos for a man she'd never seen before. The stranger looked out of place in perfectly creased jeans and a snap-front shirt that was probably fresh out of the package. Side by side, Hunter looked almost identical to Shane at that age. How could someone not question this child's paternity, especially after knowing Shane's reputation when it came to women?

Lexi had lived wondering about her son for too long. She wanted proof the boy in front of her was hers, but swore it wouldn't change anything. She needed the confirmation for her own peace of mind and sanity. Nobody else needed to know. She turned and stumbled over one of the folding chairs as she tried to escape the confines of the crowd.

"Lexi?" A strong male hand lightly touched her shoulder. "Are you all right?"

Clay Tanner. It had to be fate, Lexi thought. "If I retain your services it's illegal for you to disclose my case to anyone, right?"

"Private investigators don't have that privilege in this state, but you wouldn't have to worry." Clay ushered Lexi outside the tent and away from prying ears. "You don't have to hire me, Lex. Just tell me what you need and I assure you it will remain confidential."

"Promise me, Clay," Lexi pleaded. Her heart beat wildly in her chest. Her throat began to close, tears threatening to spill with one more blink of her eyes. "I need your help."

"You have it. Sit down before you pass out and then you'll really have some explaining to do."

Lexi looked toward the facility and the people gathered around the Langtry family, Hunter still by Shane's side.

"Tell me what you need." Clay said.

Lexi breathlessly gripped her friend's arm. "I need you to find out if Hunter's my son."

Chapter Four

"You think that boy is your son?" Clay led Lexi away from the crowd. "I think you better start from the beginning."

"I can't." Lexi frantically looked over her shoulder to double-check no one was listening. "Not here. I can't risk someone overhearing. Can we go to your place?"

Leaning into him for support, Clay protectively wrapped an arm around her and guided Lexi to her car. This was not the norm for her, Lexi thought. She prided herself on strength and perseverance no matter the obstacle. Yet twice in one day, she had found herself relying on someone else to walk her to her car. After reassuring him she was able to drive on her own, Lexi pulled out of the parking lot behind Clay's pickup.

The twenty-minute drive to Clay's gave Lexi far too much time to second-guess asking him for help. She figured shouting "Happy belated April Fool's" wouldn't fly with the detective. After keeping her secret hidden for the past thirteen years, she found the idea of unburdening it both terrifying and a relief.

Stopping behind Clay in the gravel driveway, Lexi death-gripped the steering wheel, uncertain she wanted to turn off the engine. A quick shift into Reverse seemed like a wiser option. Not giving her much of a choice, Clay strode to her car, reached across her and removed the keys from the ignition. *Damn convertibles.*

"I'm keeping these until I know you're okay." Clay sauntered to the porch. "Take your time, I'll be up here."

You can do this. Clay's the only one who can help you.

Lexi put all her trust and faith in her longtime friend, reasoning the former Alcohol, Tobacco and Firearms agent turned private investigator was a better choice than some stranger she found in the yellow pages. *Trust and faith.* A foreign concept that left a bad taste in her mouth. She trusted no one and the only thing she had faith in was her animals.

Blindly reaching for the handle, she swung the door wide, testing her footing for fear the earth would give way beneath her and swallow her whole. A part of her actually relished the idea of disappearing and not having to face the past. Slogging up the stairs, she joined Clay and slumped into one of the porch rockers.

"Are you all right?" Clay asked.

"Ask me that again an hour from now," Lexi muttered.

She laid her head back and squeezed her eyes tight, willing the courage to tell Clay about Colorado.

"How 'bout a beer?" Clay offered.

"Do you have anything stronger?"

Clay quietly laughed. "Just don't run off on me before I return."

"I can't, you took my keys," Lexi grumbled.

She drew her knees to her chest. She'd never thought she would have to explain giving up her son to anyone, let alone the father's best friend. This was her cross to bear alone and it should have remained that way forever. How would she tell her family?

How will I tell Shane?

"Lex?" Clay returned with two lowball glasses and held out one to her. "Nothing goes any further than us."

Lexi took Clay at his word. There was no other way to take him—either people confided in him with their darkest secrets or they hired him to uncover others'. But somehow, Lexi didn't think two fingers of bourbon would give her the strength she needed to come clean.

"My mom would kill me if she caught me drinking in the middle of the day." Lexi nervously laughed before tilting the glass and swallowing its contents.

"Your secret's safe with me." Unscrewing the cap, he poured her another drink before returning the bottle to the floor between them. "You realize I'm not letting you drive anytime soon."

Lexi nodded, making a mental note to call her brother Nash later and ask him to feed the horses.

"At the time I thought I was doing the responsible thing," Lexi began.

"What exactly did you do?" Clay asked.

"I had Shane's baby and gave it up for adoption."

"KEEPING IT REEL Pictures is *the* big kahuna of reality programming," Ryan boasted, steering Shane toward one of the picnic tables. "We're offering you the chance of a lifetime."

Shane listened to Ryan while he watched Clay walk Lexi to her car. Considering her earlier episode, he figured she still didn't feel well. But he was completely unprepared when Clay followed her out of the ranch and began to wonder if there wasn't more going on between the two of them. Not that he didn't trust Clay. He knew his friend would never betray him. So why did it bother him to see his best friend and his ex-girlfriend leave at the same time and look suspiciously like they were trying not to be seen together?

"You might even end up a movie star!" Hunter exclaimed enthusiastically, redirecting Shane to the conversation.

"Smart kid. Is he yours?" Ryan continued without waiting for an answer. "Look at all the reality stars turned actors. With your rodeo following you'd start off with a large fan base."

"I'm already a star and you must be aware I have an agent, right?"

"How impersonal would it be for us to go through an agent?" Ryan draped his arm around Shane's shoulder, throwing any suggestion of professionalism he had left out the window. "This is about Shane Langtry—his life, family, girlfriends, the rodeo. How much more personal can we get. This is huge! Bigger than anything else out there, and I promise, after the end of the first season, you'll be a household name."

The man definitely had his attention. Shane loved the idea of being on the tip of everyone's tongue. Stardom aside, he'd made a commitment to his family and Ride 'em High! and he wasn't about to turn his back on any of it.

"I just opened this school, I can't leave it now."

"That's the beauty of this, Shane," Ryan crooned. "We want to shoot it here."

"Here?" Shane asked.

"Wicked!" Hunter chimed in.

"Hollywood couldn't build a set this great." Ryan

swung his arms in a grand gesture. "Look at this place—
it's palatial!"

"Why are you focusing on me?" Shane asked. "I
mean I'm good but I haven't won the championship."

"The show will feature a few stars." Ryan drew an
imaginary box with his fingers. "Picture a show like
Deadliest Catch only with cowboys instead of Alaska
fishermen. People will be on the edge of their seats
watching you perform in one of America's most dangerous sports. You'll each have your own segments."

"Who else have you asked?"

"No one." Ryan shifted closer and lowered his voice.
"You're our first choice and we'd like you to be the anchor of the show."

A television offer was the last thing Shane expected
and one he wasn't quite certain his agent, Brock Hud-
son, would jump at. Why did Ryan avoid Brock, knowing he'd have to go through him at some point? With
his national rodeo sponsors, Shane was already well-
known, but the allure was almost impossible to resist.

"Is it true?" Tyler, one of the rodeo school kids, ran
up and breathlessly asked him. "Are you going to have
your own TV show?"

"Well, that didn't take long to get out." Shane shook
his head and looked down at Hunter. "What did you
do, text him?"

"Nah," Hunter laughed. "Social media is the way to
go nowadays. I tweeted it."

"I love this kid!" Ryan hugged the teen. "Your son's
a genius! Look at the buzz he's already generated here."

"Hunter's not my son," Shane said.

"Really? Could have fooled me." Ryan shrugged. "So
what do you think?"

"Excuse me, Shane," Kay interrupted. "We have someone waiting to interview us."

"Go on, I didn't mean to take up all of your time." Ryan reached out to shake Kay's hand. "That was a very moving speech up there. You raised some fine men."

"Thank you. Have we met?" Kay inquired warily.

Shane interrupted before Ryan was able to open his mouth. "I'll tell you all about it later, Mom." Shane steered Kay away from the table and nodded back to Ryan. "You'll still be around?"

"I'm not going anywhere." Ryan smiled a grin that screamed Hollywood.

"What's going on, Shane?" Kay asked. "Who was that man?"

"Mom, he could put Bridle Dance on the map."

"We are on the map—Ramblewood, Texas. There, done. Now what's this all about?"

"Here they are." An attractive brunette in jeans and red polo shirt held a microphone and directed Kay and Shane to join his brothers. "This isn't a live segment, so please don't be nervous."

"We're used to the spotlight." Shane nodded toward some of his students, who stood by watching the interview. "It's in our blood."

"It may be in your blood but it certainly isn't in mine." Kay adjusted her blouse. "I despise TV interviews. I do wish I had a mirror so I could check my makeup. In all this heat it's probably melted off."

"You look gorgeous, Mrs. Langtry." The interviewer gave a wide, overbleached smile. Some people took teeth whitening to the extreme and it bugged the hell out of Shane. Photo ready was one thing, but there was no need to be a beacon for space ships every time you opened your mouth.

"And five, four…" The woman motioned *three, two, one* with her hand. "We're here in Ramblewood with the Langtry family for the greatly anticipated opening of the Dance of Hope hippotherapy facility and the Ride 'em High! Rodeo School."

Shane listened while his mother answered the majority of the questions like a seasoned pro. If she was the least bit nervous, she certainly didn't show it. Normally Shane and Chase handled the interviews now that Cole had stepped away from the rodeo, but today belonged to their mother and Shane loved watching her take pride in their combined venture.

The interviewer posed her final question. "And with Shane getting his own reality show, you must be excited about the national publicity you'll receive."

"Shane getting his own what?"

So much for easing her into the idea.

"WHO ELSE KNOWS about this?" Clay stood in the setting sun. He was tall and tanned with a hint of sandy blond hair peeking out from under his summer Stetson. He removed his sunglasses, Caribbean-blue eyes meeting hers with all the sincerity in the world. He looked more like a movie star than a cowboy P.I.

"Only my horse, and I can trust she won't talk." Lexi attempted to laugh, rose and teetered to the porch railing that overlooked the narrow two-lane highway and emerald-green cornfields, weeks away from harvesting. It was tranquil out here, away from the bustle of her family's tourist attraction. Lexi turned to face Clay. "Now what?"

"I have to admit," Clay acknowledged, "there is a strong resemblance between the two of them, but don't jump to any conclusions until we know for certain."

"How soon can you find out?" Lexi implored, dropping back into the rocker, half the bottle gone, the effects of the bourbon beginning to take a toll. "I can't work close to him, knowing I might be inches away from my own child."

"Now that they've had the ribbon cutting, the school will do more arena work inside. It's too hot outside not to. In the meantime, I can do some digging and see what I come up with."

"And you'll find out for certain?"

"There's only one surefire way to know. You use a DNA lab for your breeding program, don't you?" Clay asked.

"Yes, but I think the Texas Veterinary Board would frown on that, let alone the ethics factor."

"Lucky for you, I don't have any ethics to worry about. I'll run the test. I can get into the bunkhouse when he's training and grab something of his."

"We're really doing this, aren't we?" Reality punched her hard in the stomach and the world began to churn in front of her.

"No more bourbon for you." Clay led Lexi inside the air-conditioned house to a couch that had seen better days. "Lay down for a while."

"My God." Lexi looked around the living room, scanning the boxes still stacked in the corners. "You've been back in town for how long and you still haven't unpacked?"

"Eh, what's another year or two?"

"Seriously." Lexi steadied herself on his arm before

flopping down on the sofa, causing a small cloud of dust to rise in the air between the two of them.

"Take my bed." Clay quickly tried to hide his embarrassment. "I'm rarely home so none of this gets used very much."

"It's fine." Lexi removed her phone from her pocket and sent Nash a quick text, feigning a vet emergency. Clay ran upstairs and returned with a pillow and a sheet before she even hit *send*.

"We all have skeletons, Lexi." He helped her stand and draped the sheet across the couch before fluffing up the pillow. Lexi lowered herself back down, tucking her legs beneath her. Clay perched on the edge of the coffee table and continued. "Some greater than others but we all have one thing we don't want anyone else to know. It doesn't make you a bad person, it makes you human. My job isn't to judge you. It's to find out if Hunter really is your son."

"You'll check out his family, too?"

"If you want me to, yes."

"I need to know he's with good people." Lexi had already decided if there were any signs of abuse or neglect she'd immediately contact an attorney and fight for her son. It was an easy decision for her to make and Lexi questioned if her maternal instincts were kicking in or if it was because Hunter looked very well taken care of, and she didn't have anything to worry about. "Then I'll figure out what to do next."

"Are you going to tell Shane?"

"I'm not going to disrupt Hunter's life for selfish reasons." If he was her son and he was happy, who was she to shatter his world? "What good can come of it? Shane already lost one son, why tell him he lost another?"

"It's your call." Clay rose and tugged all the blinds closed. "Get some sleep."

"I'm really putting you in a bad spot, aren't I?" The strain she was about to cause to Shane and Clay's friendship dawned on her. "How can you keep this a secret from Shane? If he were to ever find out you knew—"

"He'd understand I was doing my job," Clay assured her. "Lexi, I can't even begin to tell you the secrets I've had to keep."

"Thank you for understanding."

"Maybe this will make you realize you're still in love with him?" Clay said from a safe distance across the room.

"What?" Lexi snorted. "No. What? Please tell me you aren't going to play matchmaker with all of this."

"My job is to state the facts, ma'am." Clay playfully tipped his hat and left the room.

Her eyes heavy with bourbon and exhaustion, she laid her head on the pillow. The hospital room once again filled her dreams. Only this time, Shane was there, cradling their son in his arms, the way it was supposed to be.

"You're planning a reality show on Bridle Dance and you didn't discuss it with me?" Kay dragged Shane into the house practically by his ear once the interview was complete. Behind them, Cole evaded any further reality show questions from the media with a firm "no comment."

"Well, technically it wasn't my idea," Shane retorted. "The show was proposed to me and it would be filmed at the school. I haven't made any decisions so I don't see what the big deal is yet." Shane gathered his arguments. "Can you imagine the volume of business we'd bring in? Just think about the attention Dance of Hope would receive. It's a nonprofit, Mom. You'd garner all sorts of donations from across the country and we could educate people about hippotherapy."

"Slow down, will you." Kay tapped her fingers wildly on the counter. "I've seen those reality shows and they'd probably wind up victimizing the people who come here for therapy and I'll be damned if I'm going to let that happen. Most of those shows are pure trash."

"Most, not all. You used to watch some of those medical reality shows and they weren't trash." Shane argued his point knowing it was futile going up against his mother. "Why does this suddenly feel like déjà vu?"

"What are you talking about?"

"This is just like last year." Shane threw his hands in the air. "You and Cole once again opposing what I want to do. I thought we got past all of this. It would be nice at least to have a conversation before you both try to shut me down but obviously things haven't changed around here."

It had been bad enough fighting almost his entire family to open the rodeo school. If Chase hadn't stood by his side, he would have felt like a complete outsider.

"This involves all of us." Cole spoke to him in his trademark annoyingly patronizing tone. "Never mind how it will affect the students. Some parents may not approve of their kids being on television. I certainly don't want Ever involved in this."

"First, I didn't say I was going ahead with it so give me a little credit," Shane argued. "And second, we mainly teach the rodeo kids in the summer and talk about an instant career boost for them. The students over eighteen can make their own decisions."

"I wasn't finished, Shane," Cole continued. "There's a major liability factor you're not seeing."

"I haven't even had a meeting with this guy to get all the facts yet." Shane's voice strained. "I'm sure the show would cover the additional insurance and the students already have to provide their own medical insurance before they even enroll. I'd never put your daughter's reputation or anyone in this family's in jeopardy."

"I don't know, Shane." Cole took a seat at the kitchen island and folded his arms across his chest.

"I don't, either." Shane sat down next to him. "Instead of judging me or the show, let's at least hear what they have to say."

Cole agreed and Shane felt his grip on his family tighten slightly. Since their father died he felt like he was always bucking against the majority. They called it obstinacy; Shane considered it thinking outside the box.

"Have you seen what they do to the families on these shows?" Kay jutted her chin and firmly placed her hands on her hips. "They'll make all of us look like a bunch of hicks. I'm not authorizing my image or likeness."

Shane shot his brother a look, and both tried to stifle a laugh.

"What are you two giggling about?"

"Listen to you with your *image-or-likeness* talk," Shane mocked. "Hollywood's already grabbed ahold of you."

"You two have five seconds to get back outside before I pummel you both."

The grown men ran to the door. Shane called to his

mother, "Be careful, Mom, you wouldn't want that to be caught on film."

"Go on and get out of here." Kay turned and walked back into the kitchen.

"Mom?" Shane stood in the doorway. "I'm asking you to seriously consider the show. It doesn't have to be a bad thing and I think we have a shot of educating people on the rodeo and hippotherapy. It doesn't have to be all about me...not anymore."

Chapter Five

Lexi awoke to the sound of her alarm. Her head pounding, she reached out to turn it off and swiftly met with the back of the couch. For a minute, she'd forgotten where she was. Fumbling in the dark, she followed the light beaming from her phone as it played a bluesy piano riff repeatedly.

Feeling her way into Clay's kitchen, Lexi swore as she stubbed her toe on one of the many boxes stacked along the wall. "Who buys a house and never unpacks?"

Patting the wall for the switch, Lexi finally managed to turn on the lights. Silently, she searched the cabinets for a bottle of aspirin. She opened the fridge to look for something to wash it down with and found an open twelve-pack of Michelob Ultra and some individually wrapped cheese slices.

"Typical bachelor." Lexi closed the door and saw Clay standing in the doorway. "Crap! Don't scare me like that. What are you doing prowling about at this hour?"

"I might ask you the same thing, but I heard your alarm go off. Oh, and thanks for the new four-letter words even I'm unfamiliar with when you crashed into whatever it was in the living room. After that greeting, I'm officially awake for the day. Coffee? Don't answer—

it's obvious you need it. Just sit down and try not to kill yourself."

Lexi wasn't in the mood to argue with the man and a cup of strong black coffee was exactly what the doctor ordered after the amount of bourbon they drank. She watched Clay maneuver around the small, yet efficient kitchen. She'd only been in the house a few times when he first moved back to town. From the looks of things, that was yesterday. She knew Clay went through a rough patch a few years ago, and like he said, everyone had a secret. He hadn't shared his, not that she'd pushed. But glancing around the house, she realized she really didn't know much about the man any more other than what she saw on the surface. A hardworking cowboy turned detective.

"Yesterday was real, wasn't it?" In the recesses of her mind, Lexi had hoped that Hunter was another countless dream she'd had about the son she never met.

"You need to look at the flip side of this." Clay grabbed two stoneware mugs from the cabinet while he waited for the coffee to brew. "If Hunter is in fact your son, you must have some relief finally knowing how he turned out. He appears healthy and happy and that alone says he's been well taken care of.. You can't tell me you didn't wonder about that all these years."

"A day doesn't go by that I don't think of him." Lexi rubbed her eyes. "What am I going to do?"

"Nothing." Clay pulled up a chair in front of her, their knees touching. He took her hand in his and squeezed. "You asked me to help you and I will, but you need to stay out of it and let me do my job. Make your rounds at Bridle Dance and then leave. You don't have to go there every day anyway."

"Bridle Dance is my largest client." Lexi thought of

the list of horses she had to take care of on a daily basis. "I have mares ready to foal, and they've expanded the breeding program—"

"And Ashleigh is perfectly capable of checking in at the ranch for you." Clay met her gaze and held it, giving Lexi an eerie feeling he could read her mind. "Don't make excuses to stay there, Lex. Ashleigh will let you know if something needs your attention. You have other techs that can help you."

Okay, so he did read her mind. Not that she was planning on hanging around the ranch, but the thought of her son being so close she could reach out and touch him fascinated her. She wanted to learn more about Hunter and his life in Colorado. Did he have any brothers or sisters? What were his favorite foods or favorite video games? Was he involved in any other sports? She already knew he was following in Shane's footsteps, but did he follow in hers? Did he play guitar and sing like her and did he love animals? The questions churning in Lexi's head were nothing new. She asked herself at least a dozen every day, but now with Hunter so close, her mind raced with more of them.

Those questions finally had a chance of being answered and Lexi didn't want to waste a moment. But how could she get close to Hunter without raising suspicions?

"I can't stay away, Clay." Lexi steeled herself. "I've had thirteen years of wondering. If that's my son, then he has a birthday soon and I plan on celebrating with him. One way or another I'm wishing him a happy birthday."

"I HAVE TO admit, it's nice having you home in the morning." Kay bagged two dozen freshly baked apple streusel muffins and set them on the counter. "It used to be a rare occasion to wake up and see your Jeep out there."

"Yeah," Chase added. "What's going on with you? Since the school opened, you've only gone out once."

"Let's not make a federal case out of it," Shane grumbled. "We have a bunkhouse full of kids and I think it's important to be there. In fact, I think I might stay out there with them tonight. Our instructors are pulling double duty now and it's a bit much to ask every night. I also think it would be nice to include the hippotherapy kids in our marshmallow roasts. I know their bunkhouses are a way from ours, but I think it's good for all the kids to interact with one another and— What? Why are you two staring at me like that?"

"Are you feeling all right?" Kay laughed. "I was skeptical about you opening the school and spending so much time near kids, but taking up residence with them and campfires? That doesn't sound like you. You've made a point to keep your—"

Shane raised his hand to stop his mother from continuing. He had never considered himself a kid person before his involvement with Sharon, but as soon as he had held Dylan in his arms for the first time, he quickly changed his mind. When Tab took Dylan away, remembering what he'd had and lost was too hard, so Shane distanced himself from children of all ages. The further he went in his career and the more sponsors he gained, he realized how much of a role model he had become, confirmed by the fan mail he received. He had wrestled with the idea of the rodeo school for years but didn't share it with anyone. When his father died, he finally found the courage to push forward with his idea, wanting to prove to himself and his family that he was more than just a rodeo cowboy. The kids had been more fun to work with than he'd anticipated, and when they left in a few weeks, he'd actually miss them.

From day one, Shane had picked out the school's rising stars. Everyone had potential if they stuck with the sport, but the rodeo came more easily to certain kids. Usually it was because they grew up in an environment where riding was involved on a daily basis. Hunter was one of the exceptions. His family couldn't be more removed from ranch life, yet the kid's skills rivaled those of his classmate, Tyler, whose family's cattle ranch kept him in the saddle every day.

The rodeo school kids reminded Shane so much of himself at that age. Determination was written all over their faces and nothing would stop them from achieving their goals. Shane not only wanted to witness their budding careers, but he also wanted to manage them. And in a perfect world, with more hours in the day, he would.

A kid had to be careful in this business. There was someone trying to take advantage of a rookie around every corner. Luckily for Shane and his brothers, they'd had their father managing their careers when they first started out. Once they rode the circuit for a few years, they had a good sense of who was legit and who wasn't in the industry and were able to make informed decisions with their father's guidance. These kids needed that same leadership and Shane felt he was just the man for the job. Maybe someday he'd have the time, after he won the championship.

"I need to head out and wake the troops." Shane grabbed the bag of muffins from the counter. "Thanks for making these, Mom. I know the boys will appreciate it."

"You're welcome." Kay placed a hand on Shane's arm to stop him from leaving. "Muffins and good-mornings aside, don't think I've forgotten about this reality show. I meant what I said last night—I don't want any part of it."

"Point taken. And I'd never sign a contract without running it past Brock first, although I have to admit, the deal does sound intriguing."

"Let's hear them out before we make any firm decisions, Mom," Chase added. "I'm interested in finding out more about it myself. If it's legit and they don't ridicule the rodeo, then I think it has the potential of being a good thing."

"You mean lucrative." Kay smirked.

"Last I checked, lucrative was a good thing," Shane said. "But it's more than that, Mom. I worked hard designing this school and I'd like some recognition." He pushed through the screen door and bounded down the porch stairs. He welcomed the wall of heat that smacked him in the face because it was more bearable than the disappointed expression he saw when his mother looked at him some days. Shane was grateful the ribbon cutting was finally behind them so he could prove to her why he'd fought so hard for this school.

The rising temperatures made for some cranky kids and he was relieved to be able to work in a more controlled environment now that the indoor arena was open. It was one thing to be on the back of a bucking bronc in the heat where your attention was focused on the ride, another to be standing around in the sun waiting for your turn. He was all for working with kids, but hot, sweaty, willful kids crazed from heat—not so much. Especially since the majority of them came from northern states and weren't used to this weather.

Butch, one of the ranch's many border collies, greeted Shane on the walkway to the bunkhouses. Dropping the red tennis ball he perpetually carried around, the dog waited expectantly. Shane squatted down and scratched Butch behind the ears.

"What is it, boy?" Shane nuzzled the dog's neck. "You want some morning love? I think Mom needs a dog of her own to keep her company. What do you think?"

Butch wagged his tail and flopped onto his side, rolling onto his back. "How would you like to help me play a little joke on the kids this morning?" Shane rubbed the dog's white-and-black belly, triggering Butch's hind leg to kick in rhythm with Shane's ministrations.

Rising, Shane slinked toward the main bunkhouse. Giving Butch the down hand signal, the dog went into what Shane affectionately called *stealth mode* and belly-crawled along behind him as he crept silently across the porch. Shane eased the bunkhouse door open. Not only were his students ten toes up, but his on-duty den dad of an instructor was also out like a light. They were sleeping so peacefully, it would be a shame to wake them, but what fun.

Shane silently turned and grabbed a braided rope that hung from the rocking chair on the porch, and tiptoed back to the door. Raising his arm to bang the rope against the wall, Shane barely contained his laughter. Opening the door slowly, he peeked inside.

"Gotcha!" An arm reached out and tried to latch on to him. Shane scrambled and struggled to break free, yanking his own arm backward away from the grasp while Butch barked and spun around in a circle. The door swung wide and laughter poured out of the bunkhouse.

"What the—!" Shane steadied himself. "You scared the daylights out of me."

"That will teach you to sneak in here," Grant, one of his instructors, said. "We were waiting for you."

"That's not right," Shane grumbled good-naturedly. "Funny, but definitely not right."

"When do they start filming?" Hunter pushed past the other boys.

"Can we be in your show?" Tyler asked.

"Whoa, slow down, guys." Shane admired their enthusiasm but a few unanswered questions remained. Ryan's deal almost seemed too good to be true. And the fact he'd completely bypassed his agent caused Shane to wonder what the guy had left out of his proposal. "I haven't decided anything yet. Here are some muffins to hold you until breakfast. Now let's hit the gym."

Shane found it hard to concentrate on his workout alongside the boys. Two things filled his mind. He sensed something was troubling Lexi and that had kept him awake most of the night. Hell, Lexi was the only woman he'd ever said "I love you" to and would probably claim that honor until the day he died. Ryan's offer only added to his restless bed tossing.

"I'll meet you in the arena later," Shane said to Chase. "I want to check on the yearlings myself this morning."

He strode down the pathway leading from the bunkhouse toward the small outdoor satellite ranch office. Since running the ranch alongside his brothers for the past year, he felt guilty when he realized how much more Cole shouldered, so Shane and Chase could still compete and run the school. Shane offered to take on more responsibility, much to everyone's surprise, and was still struggling to find a balance. He was also learning the ropes on many aspects of the ranch and needed to review some of Bridle Dance's financial reports during his flight to South Dakota tomorrow morning to the Black Hills Roundup Rodeo. He hated to miss Fourth of July with his students, but when he'd signed on for the event, he'd thought it would be a great chance to escape for a few days. Have a little fun, ride hard and play a little harder.

His hand on the knob of the office door, he saw Lexi's convertible in the parking lot near the stables. Wanting to see how she was feeling, Shane searched the stables. When he found her, she looked like she'd spent the night in her clothes—*wasn't she wearing that shirt yesterday?* Shane stood in the shadows and watched Lexi come out of one of the stalls, slightly unsteady on her feet. Shane wondered how wild of a night she'd had with Clay. She didn't look sick, but she sure looked hung over.

"Looks like someone had a rough night."

STARTLED, LEXI WASN'T used to seeing Shane in the stables this early considering he rode out to check on the yearlings most mornings or was training for his next rodeo before the work day. Plus with the school open, she expected the students would occupy his days and probably part of his nights. Surprisingly she wondered if she'd get the chance to spend much time with him this summer. Not that they'd made plans or anything, and heaven help her if she ever said the words aloud, but Lexi was beginning to enjoy Shane's company instead of always ducking and dodging him. That is until Hunter came to the ranch and reminded her of the guilt she tried so desperately to bury.

"Cole left me a message that he sold two horses during the ribbon cutting, and the buyer wants to pick them up today. I had to swing in and do their Coggins reports before they were trailered out."

Lexi liked to save the Coggins reports for when Billy was around now that he was more familiar with the testing and reporting procedures. Wanting to heed Clay's advice, she decided to hit the stables early before there was any chance of running into Hunter. Clay told her they'd meet up later, after he had the DNA kit, so he could get a cheek swab from her and she'd write him a check for his expenses.

"You look like you were ridden hard and put away wet," Shane said. "You feeling okay? I saw you leave early with Clay yesterday."

Lexi's head shot up at the declaration. She didn't know anyone had seen them leave and she certainly hoped no one overheard their conversation.

"I wasn't feeling well. My stomach's a little off, probably some type of bug." Lexi wasn't lying at this point. Her stomach felt like it could betray her at any moment. When was the last time she ate? Clay had a pizza delivered last night, but Lexi never moved from the couch, saying she wasn't hungry. She regretted it now, along with the bourbon.

"Are you sure it's nothing more?"

Oh, no—does he know? Could he possibly?

"I have to go." Lexi brushed past him. "We'll talk later."

"It will have to be a few days from now then. I'm heading to South Dakota tomorrow morning."

"Oh." Lexi didn't think Shane would leave in the middle of his first class, but then again, it was peak rodeo season, and with Shane, the rodeo came above all else. "I hope you have a nice trip. Now, if you'll excuse me."

"Look, I'm just going to come right out and ask." Shane closed the distance between them, his eyes softening, and for a split second, Lexi thought he was going to kiss her. "Do we have a chance of a future?"

If there was any question to catch her off guard, that was the one. They'd danced around the issue since November, but never actually said the words. While the thought wasn't far from her mind, the timing was terrible.

"Shane, I—I don't know what our future holds." Lexi cleared her throat. "We just have to take things slow and see what happens."

Shane made it impossible for her to avoid meeting his gaze when he tilted her chin toward him. She'd forgotten the feel of his rough, calloused hands against her face and she'd forgotten how much she missed the way he held her and the way he would—

Shane placed both hands on either side of Lexi's face and kissed her. It was a kiss so passionate, so intense, Lexi thought she had time-warped to that fateful weekend at Devil's Thumb. Unabashed, Lexi allowed herself this one moment to remember what they'd had, to feel what they'd missed all these years.

"Don't throw away our past, Lexi."

Past. Lexi couldn't outrun the past any longer. It had caught up with her, and if Hunter proved to be her son—their son—the thought of lying to Shane for the rest of his life seemed a thousand times worse than not knowing who and where the child they created was.

Lexi broke the kiss and pushed Shane away. "What the hell do you think you're doing?"

"Tell me you don't still feel it, Lex." Shane tugged her toward him. "Since you moved home, I've endured seeing you each and every day. At Jesse's wedding we agreed to make the most of our friendship and see where it led us. You and I both knew staying away from each other would be impossible."

"You can't just kiss me whenever you feel like it," Lexi hissed. "Especially when I'm working."

"Are you honestly going to deny you have feelings for me?"

Lexi did have feelings, she did still love him, and even though her heart told her it was time to give him a second chance, the strong possibility Hunter was their son negated everything.

"Listen, Shane." Lexi jabbed at his chest. "Regardless of how or what I feel, you cannot kiss me while I'm at work, even if you do own the place! Who knows who saw that kiss? I have a reputation to maintain, so I suggest you get your butt on that plane and focus on your next ride."

"After you admit you still love me." Shane leisurely leaned against the stall door.

Lexi closed the distance between them and carefully kept her tone low so no one would overhear. "You arrogant, egotistical— How can you think for one minute—we just started—"

"Yep, I knew it." Shane slapped his thigh with his hat. "Some things never change, *mi ángel de fuego*."

Lexi was taken off guard to hear Shane refer to her as his angel of fire. The last time he'd used the nickname was before they broke up. Struggling to compose herself, she stared at him, afraid to speak.

Shane didn't share her problem. "Whenever you get

riled up like this and can't finish a thought, I know I'm right and it kills you."

If he only knew how much this all really was killing her.

Chapter Six

Shane replayed Lexi's colorful four-letter-word retort as his plane taxied down the runway the following morning. He expected nothing less from Lexi and was actually relieved to see her fiery passion unleashed. If she was feisty, she was okay and that was all that mattered.

Keep telling yourself that.

There was something definitely going on with Lexi, and as much as he hated not knowing what it was, he trusted Clay to tell him if it was serious. Trying to push all thoughts of her aside for a few hours, Shane tried to focus on the financial reports from the ranch. Truth was, he was more interested in hearing from his agent about the reality show than he was studying figures on how much grain they purchased during the second quarter of the year.

Brock told him what he knew—Keeping it Reel Pictures tended to go for more vanity-type television shows. Shane wasn't quite sure how he should take their interest in him after hearing that.

"May I get you a drink, sir?" A flight attendant interrupted his thoughts. She was cute, petite, he'd wager a natural blonde, and Shane couldn't help but notice how she leaned in closer than she should to take his order.

"Just a bottled water, please." Shane might be the wild one of the family, but he never drank before a competition. You had to be on your game at all times in that rodeo arena. The slightest mistake could cost you your life and he wasn't willing to take the chance of even having the slightest bit of alcohol in his system.

"Are you sure there's nothing else I can get for you?" the blonde asked with some added heat to her voice and an extra button undone on her blouse, emphasizing what the good Lord gave her.

She knows who I am. It amazed Shane the number of people that recognized him outside Ramblewood and away from the arena. Sure, the rodeo was big, but on a commercial flight out of San Antonio, the flight attendants were rarely local. Blondie's accent leaned more toward Bostonian and there wasn't a huge following in that part of the country.

"I'm good for now." Less than a year ago, he'd have found out if she was staying in South Dakota overnight, and if she were, he'd make damn sure she saved a horse and rode a cowboy. Now, the only person he wanted to share his bed with was Lexi, and the way that was going, he'd be collecting social security before she ever even entertained the thought. Clay was right, he might as well consider himself celibate at this point.

Checking the pulse on the side of his neck, Shane confirmed he was still alive. Silently laughing, he pulled his phone from his jeans and dialed the ranch. So much for not thinking about Lexi for a few hours.

"Hello?" Chase answered.

"Hey, how's it going there?" Shane asked.

"Pretty much the same as it was when you left," Chase said. "The house is still standing, I haven't lost a kid and men from outer space haven't beamed up the ranch."

"Okay, wise-ass." Shane smirked. "I was just checking in. Have you seen Lexi this morning?"

"And there's the real reason why you're calling." Chase laughed through the phone. "I'm surprised you didn't pass her on the way in because she got here a little after you left to check in on Crystal. Looks like it will only be a few days before she foals."

"I'm hoping I'm home before then." Shane rubbed his brow. "Dad's last foal. He would have been sleeping in the barn at this stage."

"Yeah, he would have." Chase's somber tone matched his own. "He'd be out there setting up every video camera known to man trying to capture this birth. I can hear him now—'This is going to be legendary, son. When this horse makes millions you'll thank me for recording this.' He'd get so caught up in the technology side of things, he'd probably end up missing the whole event and have to play it back to see what happened."

"Ain't that the truth." Shane swallowed his laughter for fear it might turn to tears. He missed his father greatly and he'd ride this rodeo in his honor. No matter how old Shane had been, Joe had always accompanied him to the Black Hills Roundup. This was the first year he was going alone.

"I should've signed up with you this year," Chase said. "The school could have managed without us for a few days. You know Dad's there in spirit with you and he'd be proud of everything we've accomplished this past year."

"Thanks, bro." Shane swallowed, trying to clear the lump forming in his throat. "I think I really needed to hear that today. And don't sweat not being here. Those kids need you more than I do."

"Speaking of such, the boys are waiting for me," Chase said. "Enjoy your flight, don't wear out the flight attendants and call me later. Oh, that's right, you only have eyes for Lexi now. Forget about her while you're there and focus on your ride."

"Thanks, I will." Shane turned off his phone and pocketed it. Easing the seat back a little, he checked his watch.

"Your water, Mr. Langtry."

"Any idea when we'll be taking off?"

"It should only be a few more minutes. We've had some congestion this morning. Good luck on your ride tonight."

The last two words were heavy with innuendo, confirming she knew exactly who he was and hadn't just read his name on the flight manifest. Shane was flattered, but nope, still not interested. He wanted to get this show over with, meet with his sponsors and get home.

Leaving never bothered him before now. He chalked it up to Crystal's foal and the rodeo school. The boys had a lot to learn during their monthlong stay, and while he knew they were in more than capable hands with Chase, Kyle and the other instructors they'd brought in, he'd have felt better if he was there, too. Hell, even Cole had offered to throw his hat in the ring for a few sessions.

And why not? The Langtry brothers were the main draw to the Ride 'em High! Rodeo School. They were a package deal, and if someone was going to spend that amount of money for instruction, they felt better knowing a trio of rodeo champs were there to show them how it was done.

And once the reality show started taping—correction, *if* the reality show started taping—he wondered how many endorsement deals would come out of it. He'd already had a few from saddle makers, a boot company and other equipment manufacturers, but Shane wanted a nationwide truck campaign under his belt and then he could say he'd truly arrived.

Hunter was the one student he was most sure of—the boy was strong, independent and extremely competitive—and he had the drive needed to succeed. He was more mature than some of the older boys, a maturity Shane definitely didn't have at that age. The kid had the potential to go far in this business and Shane still debated whether or not to tell his agent about him. It was probably best to discuss it further with his parents when they arrived for Family Day.

"Just five more months and maybe it will all be mine."

"Excuse me?"

Shane hadn't realized he'd said the words out loud. He coolly glanced at the man across the aisle. "I'm competing in a rodeo tonight and I'm vying to win the world all-around rodeo champion title at the National Finals in December."

The man stared at him as if Shane were speaking in tongues, then turned back to his paper. *Clearly not a fan.* The plane began to move and the flight attendant picked up the in-cabin phone and began her announcements, rarely breaking eye contact with him.

Shane closed his eyes and rested his head against the seat. Lexi and yesterday's kiss came to mind. He couldn't get the woman out of his head, regardless of who he was with. For the past thirteen and a half years, whenever he closed his eyes, she was there. No one compared to Lexi, and no matter how hard he tried, no one ever would.

WITH SHANE AWAY, Lexi felt a little more at ease around the stables, especially since she now didn't have to worry about him kissing her randomly. She walked out of the barn and started toward her car, having avoided everyone from the rodeo school. Lexi knew she needed to keep her distance, and whether Hunter turned out to be her son or not, she had made the decision to give her child to another family a long time ago. There was no going back and Lexi was beginning to question if discovering the truth was wise.

"Done for the day, dear?" Kay asked, walking toward her on the path from Dance of Hope.

"Short list today," Lexi said. "Just an insemination—everything else looks good. Crystal's close, though. She's dripping milk this morning so I give it two days at the most."

"I never did understand this artificial insemination thing. I know it's safer for the horse, but do you ever feel like you're playing God?"

"Most definitely," Lexi agreed. "I'll breed them but I don't want to get involved in genetically altering horses. It's too risky for me."

"I wanted to talk to you for a minute. Can you come in for a cup of coffee?"

Lexi sent Ashleigh and Billy ahead to the next ranch and followed Kay into the house. Lexi adored the Langtry home, especially the kitchen. With its open floor plan and use of natural log construction, the house had a cozy atmosphere, despite its vastness. The rooms were defined with the use of oversize furniture and you felt comfortable no matter where you were.

Kay popped a couple of pods into the Keurig coffee-maker and within a minute had two piping cups of coffee. Setting the creamer out, she joined Lexi at the table.

"I just love that machine. I wish we had one when Joe was alive. That man always had to have a fresh pot of coffee. Not like he wasn't capable of making it himself, he just always had me do it. You know how men can be. Listen to me ramble on. I need a favor and I want you to keep it between us for now."

"Sure." There was no telling what the Langtry matriarch had up her sleeve. Lexi had heard stories of her wild younger years. The woman was free-spirited and gutsy, and there wasn't much she hadn't tackled in her day.

"My house is getting empty. Two of my boys are married, the other two are hardly ever home, and now that Joe's gone, I'm feeling a little lonely in this big place. Shane hinted a few times that I need a dog, although I think he's implying one of the ranch dogs. Don't get me wrong, I love border collies, but I have a particular dog in mind."

"I think that's wonderful." A dog would be the perfect companion for Kay, filling the void she must feel, always coming home to an empty house. "What breed are you considering?"

"Last week when I was in town, I saw Penny and Bella, that beautiful 'parti' poodle of hers. Those partis always remind me of our paint horses. Well, anyway, Penny told me that Bella's mom had her second litter and one of the puppies was jet-black. It was the only puppy not spoken for and, Lexi, when I stopped over and saw that little black fuzz ball, I felt this instant connection."

"A standard poodle is a lot of work with regular grooming every few weeks," Lexi said. "But you wouldn't have to worry about shedding. I'm assuming this is going to be an indoor dog."

"I already downloaded a bunch of poodle books to my computer. And Penny would be his groomer. Do you want to see a picture of him?"

Kay was adorable in her enthusiasm over the dog. If she had the patience to raise four surly cowboys and look after a husband, then owning a poodle would be a cakewalk.

"I didn't want that shedding like we had with Chinook." Kay flipped through the photos on her iPhone, finally finding the one she wanted. "Loved the dog, but I swear some nights I went to bed with fur-covered eyeballs."

Lexi fondly remembered the Langtrys' husky and Joe's best friend. "Oh, this puppy is so precious."

"I've already named him Barney, and I know you're an equine vet, but if you have a chance tonight, would you be able to go and see him with me…just to check him out and make sure he's okay? The breeder said the puppies have been weaned and some are already gone."

"I love the name Barney, and yes, I will be happy to go with you tonight. I'll give you a call after I finish my rounds and we'll head out then. But why don't you want anyone to know about it?"

"My boys will give me one hell of a ribbing when they hear I want a poodle. I'd rather wait and surprise them with it."

"I don't see why they'd tease you. They're big sturdy dogs and I can't see you being the type to have one running around in a show cut, so he'll just look like a curly-coated retriever. I think it's the perfect choice and poodles are one of the most intelligent breeds."

Lexi checked her watch. It was almost lunchtime and she needed to catch up with Ashleigh and Billy at her next appointment. Kay walked Lexi outside and the sound of laughter spilled across the road as the Ride 'em High! class ran past on the way to the bunkhouse kitchen.

Hunter's voice rose above the crowd. It wasn't because it was louder or stronger, but because Lexi instinctively tuned in to listen just for him.

"They are a proud bunch, aren't they?" Kay looked toward the crew. "Remind me so much of my boys when they were that age, running around here all full of the rodeo. And all you girls, so sweet on them."

Kay immediately looked to Lexi. "I'm sorry. Me and my big mouth."

"It was a long time ago." Lexi croaked out the words. Almost as if he read her mind, Hunter turned to look in her direction. Their eyes met and he waved.

His smile was akin to looking in a mirror. How could anyone else not see Hunter was Shane's and her child? She quickly turned to Kay, who was studying her. Did she know?

"What's bothering you, Lexi?" Kay asked. "You've been very pensive the past few days."

Lexi wanted to follow Hunter. She wanted to sit next to him at lunch and find out his favorite foods, what music he listened to, how he was doing in school, what his family was like. *Family.* He wasn't her family anymore. She made the choice to put Hunter before herself a long time ago and she didn't regret it.

Lexi looked to Kay. "Thank you for worrying about

me, but I'm fine. I'll call you later and we'll go see Barney."

Lexi forced herself to walk toward her car instead of the path leading to the bunkhouses. *Don't look back.* Nothing good came from regrets except more regrets.

THE WEATHER IN Belle Fourche, South Dakota, was warm but still a far cry from the sweltering heat of Ramblewood. Although it was located in the heart of the country, Belle Fourche resembled most small Texas towns. Main Street wasn't unlike Ramblewood's own and soon there would be a cattle drive coming down this one to kick off the Black Hills Roundup festivities.

Downtown, the carnival silently awaited the setting sun, when lights would twinkle in the calliope-filled air, enticing tourists to partake in its magical charms. Cowboys and cowgirls from across the nation anxiously awaited the competition of one of the oldest outdoor rodeos. Shane could still picture his father with a foam cup of coffee in one hand and a camera in the other, photographing the entire scene. Despite the crowds, the streets seemed empty without Joe by his side.

Knowing the Black Hills Roundup was one of Tab's favorite rodeos, Shane scanned the area for Dylan as he always did at this event. Even though Tab distanced himself from the rodeo shortly after gaining full custody, Shane figured he'd still bring his son around. Years had gone by and Shane hadn't seen or heard a word about him. This event was a part of who Tab was and all fathers wanted their children to know where they came from, didn't they?

A string of Miss Rodeo South Dakota contestants posed for photos around the large stone compass marking the geographical center of the country. It always bugged his father that the true center of the country was thirteen miles north of here. Another fond memory. Belle Fourche had been their father-and-son time and the pain of his loss was more raw than Shane imagined it would be.

After checking into his hotel, he called his agent.

"Keep in mind, these are the same people who produced *Malibu Beach*," Brock said through the phone. "Yes, they took unknowns and made them millionaires, but they are also laughingstocks who no one will ever take seriously. That's not what I want for one of my clients. Money shouldn't be the driving force here. You have plenty of that. Fame, yes—go for the fame—but make sure it's the type of fame you want. And I promise you, once you sign, there will be scripts involved and some little piss-ass director telling you to pick fights with your brothers just to raise the ratings. Reality shows are anything but real and I'm advising you not to accept this offer."

Not the words Shane expected to hear from Brock, but he respected the man's honesty. He knew some of the shows were scripted and he wasn't about to let anyone treat him like a trained monkey.

"I'm not making any decisions tonight," Shane said. "I understand the impact it will have on my family and maybe it should be filmed on the road and not at Bridle Dance."

"I don't mean to sound harsh," Brock said. "But do you honestly think they'd still want you if the ranch, the school and the family weren't involved?"

"Ryan said I was the anchor of the show."

"Because you're wealthy," Brock said. "And they will

find a way to use that against you. Your friends on the circuit will become your enemies when they *suddenly appear* at Ride 'em High! because the producers brought them there to create conflict. Without conflict, there's no show."

"Is there any good side to this?" Shane almost regretted asking. "If it was all bad, none of these shows would exist."

"Only the money and the fame, if you can call it that. Keeping it Reel Pictures doesn't produce quality. They're all about quantity at the cheapest cost. They can make a mint off of you and the only money you'll see is from people paying you to make appearances."

"I'm already paid to make appearances."

"And that right there is the reason they went directly to you instead of me. A show like this may not sit well with some of your sponsors and you're pulling in a nice chunk of change with them. Your popularity increased tenfold with the boot company, and if you lose a sponsorship like that, you have to carry everything on yourself. Your money isn't endless. I want the best for you, Shane, and trust me, this isn't it. I'm assuming you're still meeting with your sponsors for publicity shots tomorrow."

Shane listened to his agent for a few more minutes before ending the conversation. He promised to discuss it with his family. He needed a clear head and he needed something other than airline almonds in his stomach.

He pulled in front the Belle Inn Restaurant. It didn't look like much from the outside but the food was as close to home as he could get.

"What can I do you for, cowboy?" a waitress greeted him.

"Aw, shucks, I bet you say that to all the men around

here." Normally he would have been attracted to her more-than-generous curves but women who tried too hard to be sexy no longer held any appeal. He preferred Lexi's "this is who I am, so deal with it" attitude. Hell, she'd look sexy wearing a feed bag.

"Yep, sure do," she said. "Especially when I have hundreds of them coming through the door. Now come on, hon, tell me what you want to order."

Shot down and I wasn't even trying!

Shane ordered and wondered how things were going at the ranch. *What is wrong with you?* This was his time away from family and work and commitments—his time to be free and do whatever he damn well pleased.

Oh, my god! I'm homesick.

By EARLY EVENING, Lexi found herself back on the ranch, watching a black standard poodle puppy scamper across the porch.

"He's definitely going to be a big one judging by the size of his feet." Lexi tapped her fingers on the floorboards for Barney to chase. Running to Kay, he tested his strength by nibbling on her thumb. "Watch out for those needle teeth. They'll—"

"Ouch!" Kay snatched her hand away from Barney's clutches.

"—get you." Lexi watched Kay's expression light up when the puppy stretched for another go at her hands, forcing her to sit on them. "I think you two are going to be very happy together. Just don't let him near the other animals until he gets the rest of his shots."

"Can you do that?" Kay asked.

"I could, but I think you should establish a relationship with Dr. Cerf so Barney gets used to going to the vet and socializing. Plus he needs to get used to riding in the car and visiting with people off the ranch. It will be good for him."

"I think it's time for a potty break." Kay rose, swooping the puppy up in her arms. "When Chinook was a puppy I made a point of taking her out every hour and we had very few accidents. Come to think of it, the boys had more accidents than the dog did."

Lexi was sure of that. Why the woman didn't have a head of solid white hair baffled Lexi. Then again, Nice 'n Easy did amazing things. She handed Kay the leash from the porch floor, and Kay snapped it on Barney's collar and walked down the stairs. Lexi followed her into the side yard, away from the massive vegetable garden.

"Looks like we have company." Kay nodded toward the pathway.

Chase and a few of the boys walked toward them.

"What do we have here?" Chase asked, crouching down in the grass. Barney bounced straight at them.

"Meet Barney, the newest member of our family." Kay beamed.

"You got a dog?" Chase asked. "I think that's great, Mom. And isn't he a cutie. What is he?"

"He's a standard poodle," Kay replied.

Kay and Chase continued to talk but the words faded away. Hunter stood in front of Lexi, close enough for her to reach out and touch him, hug him, never let him—no! She purposely didn't hold her baby after she gave birth, knowing it would be a pain too deep to bear. Hunter squatted next to Chase and ran his hand over the puppy's head.

"I miss my dogs," Hunter said.

Lexi was unable to draw herself away from him. "How many do you have?"

"Three." Hunter's gaze never left Barney. He continued to pet and play with the dog. "Mom has a Westie, Dad has a schnauzer and me and my brother and sister have a Jack Russell named Jack." He laughed, meeting her eyes. "I know, real creative."

The words *Mom* and *Dad* stung for a moment, then quickly passed when Lexi envisioned him with his family. Her son had siblings and pets.

"How old are your brother and sister?" Lexi knew that the couple who adopted her son didn't have any other children at the time.

"My sister's five and my brother's eleven."

They were younger—one more sign this was her child.

"We were just headed out to the store to get some s'mores fixings," Chase said.

"Can I stay?" Hunter asked, seated cross-legged in the grass with the puppy in his lap.

Chase looked to his mother for approval.

"It's fine." Kay nodded. "We'll be here when you get back."

Silently Lexi screamed for joy and prayed Chase would make this the longest grocery-store trip in history. She watched the way Hunter's hand stroked Barney's chubby puppy belly. He talked softly to the dog, welcoming him to his new home and telling him how much he'd like living there.

"I can remember when Shane was younger, he wanted to be present for every foal born on this ranch, just like his father," Kay began, reaching out and scratching Barney under the chin. "Shane and Joe sat in those stables all night long and watched the mares, not going to bed until each foal was able to stand on their own. You remind me a lot of Shane—you have that caring nature in you, too."

Lexi mentally snapped a photo of grandmother and grandson, side by side—the way it should be. The way it couldn't be.

AFTER A SUCCESSFUL ride, Shane made it to the hotel for a hot shower followed by a couple of interviews and a meeting with one of his sponsors. His back still ached thanks to the final unanticipated twist the bronc had thrown in at the last second. Regardless, he held on to his first-place standing. He had a full schedule of events throughout the summer, and he usually looked forward to each and every one of them. This was his life, this was in his blood…this was not where he wanted to be tonight.

Stepping out into the hallway, Shane almost collided with a room service waiter. When he made his way around the cart, he got a glimpse of a tall blond cowboy turning the corner toward the elevators. *Tab Fanning?*

He ran to catch up with him before the doors closed, but by the time he reached the elevator, the cowboy was gone. As he raced down the adjacent stairwell, the leather soles of his boots almost slipped on the painted steps. At the bottom, with his heart in check, he took a deep breath before he turned the knob and walked into the lobby.

The elevator was on its way back up, meaning Tab— if it was Tab—had already gotten off. Not seeing him, Shane ran out on the sidewalk. Scanning the crowds of tourists and cowboys, he tried to spot the man he had seen only moments ago. Almost a head taller than most of the people around him, Shane spied him across the street.

"Hey, Shane, we have to meet with another sponsor." One of his teammates grabbed his arm and tried to lead him inside. "We're running behind, man, come on."

After waiting all these years to find out how Dylan was doing, he wasn't about to let the opportunity pass him by.

"Tell them I had an emergency and I'll be there soon." It was a stretch but not much of one. To Shane, this was a sanity emergency.

Down the street, the carnival was in full swing. Lights loosely hung in front of the games impossible to win. The carousel turned counterclockwise while horses and tigers slowly dipped and bobbed in time with the music. The scent of greasy funnel cakes and salty popcorn permeated the evening air. Shane once again searched the face of every man, hoping one of them was Tab. Finally he recognized the man he'd seen in the hotel. Shane ran to catch up to the cowboy and called out his name.

"Tab. Is that you?"

Time had weathered him some, but this was still the same man who had taken away the son he'd thought was his.

"Shane," Tab said flatly. "I had a feeling I might run into you here."

"The last I heard you retired." Shane looked past Tab to see if Dylan was near. "Are you alone?"

"Dylan has expressed an interest in the rodeo, more than I wanted him to. I told him he could pick one rodeo this summer and of course he had to choose one of my favorites."

"The rodeo's in his blood. Where is he?" Shane asked, eager to see the young man he'd become. "I'd love to say hello."

"Shane." Tab removed his hat and moved off the sidewalk, allowing a group of people to pass. "Dylan doesn't have any recollection of who you are. He was a baby when he left, and while I appreciate everything you did for *my son,* I think it's best to leave the past alone."

Shane knew the chances of Dylan remembering him were slim but there had always been hope. Until today.

"Honey." A gorgeous brunette approached Tab and snaked an arm around his waist. "The kids and I are getting hungry."

Behind her three kids playfully wrestled with each other as they made their way toward the adults.

"Come on, Dad." The oldest boy stood next to the woman. "There's a pizza stand over there."

"Wendy, this is an old friend of mine, Shane Langtry." Tab nodded to Shane. "Shane, this is my wife and kids, Dylan, Sandy and Will."

"Did you know my dad when he was in the rodeo?" the oldest boy asked. Dylan had grown into a fine young man—a teenager this year. Shane wouldn't have recognized him if he'd smacked into him. The chipmunk cheeks and baby pudge had been replaced by the long and lean form of his father.

"I did," Shane choked out. "He was my toughest competition. I don't want to keep you from your family. It was good seeing you, Tab…ma'am." Shane tipped his hat to Wendy and turned toward the hotel. Forcing himself not to look back, he tried to will the tears from his eyes.

Focus, Shane. Meet with the sponsors, make your next ride and get the hell out of here.

Chapter Seven

Miranda and Jesse's Fourth of July picnic should have been Lexi's escape, considering the amount of help Miranda needed this year. Lexi knew how difficult it was to move about once you reached the end of your pregnancy, especially in the summer. And carrying twins didn't make things any easier.

Jesse was adorable, waiting on his wife, hand and foot, making sure she didn't do anything except "sit pretty and give orders." The ornery cowboy bowing to his wife's every wish was a sight to behold. Fifty years from today, they'd probably sit on the same porch, watching their grandkids plan this picnic.

The Ride 'em High! kids and Dance of Hope hippotherapy families were some of the first people to arrive and immediately started to set up for one of their birthdays. It was nice to see the children from both facilities interact with each other. Joe would have been so proud of his boys.

Lexi hoped to spend more time around Hunter this afternoon. Yesterday had been an unexpected gift. She'd learned how much he loved his family and school, that he played football and was an Xbox addict. The more he spoke, the more she saw bits and pieces of her and

Shane. Even without a DNA test, there was no doubt Hunter was her child.

She tried to convince herself not to come to the picnic. It would be best for her and Hunter if she stayed away. Clay had warned her and she should have heeded his advice. The harder she tried to keep away, the more she reasoned with herself why only one more day wouldn't hurt. One more day meant a few more questions answered. One more day became two and Lexi didn't know how she would be able to say goodbye.

Any remote possibility of telling Shane and Hunter's adoptive parents the truth was out of the question after having spoken with Hunter yesterday. He and his parents had an amazing life together and she saw no reason to disrupt it. Why hurt Shane with the truth only to have his son leave for home in a few weeks? Lexi had lived this long not knowing a single thing about her son. Now that she did, she'd have to be satisfied and let Hunter go back to his own life. With his talent, she was sure to see him again…from a distance.

"Hang in there just another few days and we'll know the truth," Clay said over her shoulder.

"When did you get his sample?" Lexi looked up at him, the hint of a summer breeze swirling the humidity around her instead of relieving the heat.

"A few days ago when you were kissing Shane in the stables."

"How did you know about that?" Lexi didn't remember seeing his truck on the ranch that day.

"Because I was there getting strands from his hairbrush and on my way out I saw you. Luckily he's still at an age where his mom—sorry, his adoptive mom—writes his name on everything. And don't look at me that way. I can get in and out of places and you'd never have a clue I was there, which apparently was the case when I swung by the ranch yesterday to see Cole and saw you and Hunter together. Lexi, you need to keep your distance from him."

"He came to me," Lexi argued.

"And your legs were broken, forcing you to stay on the ground, next to him."

"You don't have the slightest clue how it feels to be inches away from your own child—a child perpetually on your mind." The baby she ran from so many years ago had found her and there was no way in hell she was letting him go this time. It wasn't healthy and she knew it, but it felt amazing to be near him. "Once I know for certain, I'll be able to walk away."

"You're sure you'll be able to?" Clay asked.

"I never expected to see him again." Lexi watched Miranda's almost full-grown bloodhounds, Rhett and Scarlett, chase Hunter and the other boys around the field of wildflowers.

Clay eyed her suspiciously. "I have an associate in the Denver area doing recon on the Rathbones' house and so far they seem to be a normal family."

Lexi continued to observe Hunter from a distance for the remainder of the day, choosing to stay close to her own family. Tradition dictated everyone bring a dish to share, but Mazie had brought, at last count, thirteen different offerings. When Lexi showed up empty-handed, her mother assured her she was covered.

"Okay, spill the beans." Mazie slid in next to her on the picnic bench. "Rumor has it you spent the night with Clay Tanner."

"What?"

"Don't deny it." Mazie waggled a finger at her. "Your car was there all night and into the morning."

"You told me you had an emergency." Her brother, Nash, jumped into the conversation. "You and the P.I.? Now I know what kind of undercover work he does."

"It's not what you think." On the verge of a short circuit, Lexi's brain tried to find an excuse. "I did have an emergency and then Clay called and asked me to check on Dream Catcher. We got to talking and drinking and it was just safer if I spent the night on his couch."

It was half-true, at least. Lexi wondered how many other people at the picnic were having this same conversation with Clay. Acknowledging a rumor even existed was enough to fuel it further. But this one was different. She didn't want Shane to think she'd sleep with his best friend. Lexi had had her cruel moments over the years, but crossing such a line was beneath her.

"How did his *investigation* go?" Mazie teased.

"Okay, more than I want to know." Nash made a disgusted face and stood up from the table. "At least you chose a good guy this time instead of those lowlifes you usually end up with."

"I didn't choose anyone and, Mazie, please stop this rumor before it gets out of control. You have a big mouth, put it to good use."

"That wasn't very nice," Mazie responded with a pout.

"I didn't mean it in a bad way. But you are the gossip queen and you know it. I'm asking you to spread the word about how untrue the rumor is."

Mazie contemplated her request for a minute. "There really isn't anything going on between you two?"

Lexi shook her head. "No and there won't be."

Not wanting to be the topic of party conversation, Lexi thanked Jesse and Miranda and decided to call it a night. Elvis Watts and his band began to play another set when something caught her eye on stage.

"Hello, Ramblewood!" Elvis boomed over the microphone. "We have a young guest star up here who's going to sing us some old-school Johnny Cash."

Hunter made his way to the microphone, a Les Paul guitar in hand. Slipping the strap over his shoulder, he played the first few notes of "Folsom Prison Blues" and stopped. A crowd quickly gathered in front of the stage and cheered. Teasing them again, he played the same beginning riff.

"Who wants to hear a little Johnny tonight?" Hunter leaned into the microphone and grabbed it with one hand, angling the stand toward him. Looking to the band, he said, "Think we should give them what they want?"

Elvis laughed and nodded, obviously enjoying Hunter's showmanship.

"Let's do this." Hunter counted the band down and they began to play.

Captivated by his voice and proud of his talent, Lexi watched Hunter play until her heart was about to burst. She needed to leave before she started shouting "That's my incredible son up there!" She needed to get away and fast.

"Where are you going?" Mazie called after her.

"The fireworks are going to start soon and I want to get back home and make sure the horses aren't spooked." Many of the ranches piped music through the stables during Fourth of July celebrations to cover the cracking of the fireworks, which sounded like gunshots. Autumn wasn't a fan of loud noises and Lexi wanted to make sure someone left a radio playing before the first blast. "Tell Mom and Dad I have everything covered at the farm. There's no need for you all to miss the fireworks."

Once she arrived on the Lawson farm, Lexi ran through the barn until she reached Autumn. Wrapping her arms around the horse's neck, she wept against her mane.

"What have I done?" she asked the mare. "I gave away my child, my only child, and now I can't even tell him how proud I am of him."

WATCHING THE FIREWORKS from the airplane was a new experience for Shane. Still in the lead, he'd decided to cut out of the roundup early and head home. By the time morning rolled around, Shane was certain his agent would have his hide for leaving before sponsor photos were taken, but he didn't care.

He wanted to get home and tell his mom about Dylan. Despite their differences over the past year, Shane knew she'd be the one person who'd always be there for him. No matter how old he was, there were some days only a mother could make better.

When his plane touched down, there was a message from Chase telling him Crystal was beginning to foal. Shane retrieved his Jeep from the long term parking lot and sat in the holiday traffic for the next two hours before finally reaching the ranch. It was almost midnight when he pulled into the parking lot. The stables were aglow and the grounds bustled with activity in anticipation of Joe's dream foal. Why was it that a foal arriving in the middle of the night seemed more the norm than during daylight hours?

Inside the stables, his family and the rodeo school students quietly gathered outside Crystal's stall. Shane peered through the door and saw the mare lying on her side in the middle of a contraction. Ashleigh and Billy stood nearby but he didn't see Lexi.

Expecting his question, Ashleigh said, "She's on her way."

The sound of fast footfalls caused them all to turn toward Lexi running down the hallway. Even in old jeans, a T-shirt and ratty sneakers she looked beautiful.

"How are we doing?" Lexi quickly tied her hair up in a bun while she listened to Ashleigh's report. Turning to face everyone, Lexi motioned them all closer. "I need you all to join hands while we have a moment of silence to remember the man that put this foal's life in motion. Joe, I know you're watching over us."

"WHAT ARE YOU doing home so early?" Kay hugged her son. "I thought you were staying until tomorrow."

"Change in plans." Shane caught Lexi watching him before she quickly returned her attention to the foal. Her eyes were puffy and her nose slightly red. He wondered if she'd been crying before she arrived.

After several contractions, Crystal expelled a gush of fluid. There were a few oohs and aahs, and one "wicked" that sounded like it came from Hunter. Straining to check her back end, the horse tried in vain to stand. Another contraction racked her body, and the beginnings of the sac appeared.

"I see something." Hunter pointed to the mare's raised tail.

"That's the amniotic sac," Lexi said. "It protects the foal inside the mother."

What appeared to be a white hoof and leg emerged when Crystal once again attempted to stand. Breathing heavy, the horse met Shane's eyes and held them. Lying back on her side, she grunted and pushed again, the room becoming quiet except for the mare's ragged breaths.

Another leg appeared and Lexi entered the stall, bending down to see what she could of the foal. Tearing the sac open with her hands, she grabbed hold of the pure white legs. After several minutes, she looked to Shane for help.

He noiselessly entered the stall, not wanting to startle the mare. He firmly gripped the foal's front legs and tugged while Crystal lay there motionless, letting him help her. The white head emerged and Lexi quickly cleared the sac from the foal's mouth while Shane continued to pull. When the body was halfway out, Shane tugged again on the foal's legs.

Lexi quickly checked the mare. "She's showing signs of distress. We need to get this foal out now."

"Is this a—"

"Don't, Shane." Lexi stopped him from saying the two words any breeder dreaded to hear. "On the count of three." Lexi took one of the horse's legs while Shane wrapped both hands around the other.

"One, two…" On three, the foal slid from the mare's body. Lexi pulled it slightly to the side, wanting the umbilical cord to break naturally. Shane stripped away the rest of the sac while an exhausted Crystal lifted her head to watch.

Stepping aside, they looked down at the pure white foal while it lifted its head and struggled to roll onto its chest.

Gasps came from the hallway.

"Oh, heavens, no," Kay said.

It was their greatest fear. A lethal white horse.

THE BARN WAS in a panic. Not all pure white horses with blue eyes were afflicted with lethal white syndrome and Lexi hoped this was one of those cases. When breeding American paints, there was always the risk, one Lexi tried to eliminate by always performing a detailed lineage background check and genetic testing before she bred any horse.

Shane sat on the stall floor, cradling the foal's head in his lap and wiping its nose and mouth. *Almost thirteen years ago to the day, he should have been cradling Hunter.* Lexi dressed the broken umbilical cord and they left mother and foal to bond while they cleaned themselves up. After an hour, Crystal began to show signs of rejecting her baby. Time was not in their favor. Lethal whites were born missing sections of their intestines and began to die within hours of birth. It was a painful death and one where euthanasia was the only humane option.

Thirty minutes later the foal still hadn't stood and Lexi feared the first signs of colic were beginning to appear. Ignoring the crowd that still gathered in the hallway, she gently opened the stall door and went inside. Shane joined her, and when she crouched down next to the foal, he squeezed her hand, wordlessly begging her to save the newborn.

Lexi placed her stethoscope against the horse and listened for signs of distress. He appeared weak but not in any pain, and with Shane's help, she was able to get the foal to stand. Lexi usually frowned upon most foal interference, fearing it would strain the foal's tendons or impede the important bonding time. But after a wobbly half hour, he managed to stay upright on his own.

The foal passed the usual reflex tests and Lexi wanted to see if he would nurse on his own. When Crystal became agitated and started violently kicking her baby, Lexi knew she had to separate them and asked Billy to take Crystal into a neighboring stall. Lexi ran her hands over the animal's coat and pink skin under the overhead lights. Uncertain if her eyes were playing tricks on her, Lexi swore she saw lighter patches of white within the coat. Two different shades of white would mean the horse was a dominant white, and not a lethal. Nothing would make her happier at the moment. Unless you counted reversing the hands of time and asking for a do-over.

Ashleigh prepared the milk replacer while Lexi attempted to milk Crystal without getting herself kicked. The colostrum contained the necessary antibodies to protect the foal from infection, providing the horse lived. They had an emergency reserve of frozen colostrum, but Lexi always wanted to try every option to get the mother's before she went that route.

"Let's see if we can get this boy to eat." Lexi felt all eyes were on her but she directed her words to Shane. She knew how much this horse meant to him and the rest of the Langtry family. If the foal readily accepted the milk replacer, it was another good sign. "It takes around twelve hours for the signs of lethal white syndrome to show. I'll be right here with you."

While Ashleigh fed the foal, Lexi ran outside to grab her strap-on headlamp from the car. She'd been wrestling with telling Shane the truth about their child when she received the call to come to the barn. Shocked to see him there, Lexi knew she had to push any thoughts of him and Hunter aside and focus on the potentially devastating situation inside. On the way back to the stables, Hunter met her outside the doors.

"Is he going to die?" he asked.

"I don't know." The moment felt surreal. Hunter was, in all likelihood, her son, and he was looking to her for answers about the foal. "I'm not a hundred percent sure he's a lethal white horse."

Hunter shook his head and looked at his bare feet. "Everyone was excited when he was being born. It was sick…well, kind of gross, but a sick gross. I don't understand why everyone's upset he's an albino. Why are you calling him a lethal white?"

Lexi sat on the wrought-iron bench outside the stable entrance and patted the spot next to her. Explaining the hardships of genetics and the lack of control over the situation wasn't easy with adults, even harder with children. But Hunter was almost a teenager and Lexi felt he could handle the truth. His parents might feel otherwise, but she didn't want to lie to him. She noticed Billy standing in the doorway, and while he was six years older than Hunter, this was probably confusing to him as well.

Motioning for Billy to join them, Lexi tried her best to explain the situation.

"A lethal white is different from an albino. A horse with overo lethal white syndrome usually has blue or gray eyes, but it's a genetic condition where both parents carry the defective gene. If this foal does have it, he will have an underdeveloped digestive tract and will not be able to pass anything. Surgery has never been successful, and within hours, he'll show signs of colic and cramping and will have to be put down."

"I thought we did genetic testing before we bred them," Billy said.

"We did, and these horses have been DNA tested for that gene. The problem is, American Paints are one of the breeds this syndrome runs in, and many of the Bridle Dance horses are the frame-overo color pattern, where the base is any color, but they have irregular white patches and many have bald faces. Even with testing, there is still a rare possibility that one will carry the mutation. Keep in mind this foal's parents don't belong to us, and if this is a lethal white, neither one can be bred again."

"But you said you weren't sure if this horse was a lethal white," Hunter said.

"That's why I came out to get this." Lexi held out her hand and showed Hunter the strap of her headlamp. "This will help me see his coat and skin clearer so I can get a better idea. I thought I saw a slight pattern to his coat, and if that's the case, then we may have a horse that's considered dominant white. The true test is if our foal passes the milk replacer we gave him."

Hunter nodded at her words and she knew it was a lot for him to absorb. Billy wasn't convincing in his stoicism, and she feared he might break at any given moment. She knew he had a strong love for horses, but in this field, you had to be able to take the good with the bad, or else you'd never make it.

"I think everyone should call it a night." Lexi rose, fighting the urge to wrap her arms around Hunter and tell him everything was all right. But it might not be and Lexi feared if she touched him, she wouldn't be able to let go when the time came for him to return home to his family. "Shane and I will stay with the foal all night."

"I want to stay." Billy squared his shoulders, confident and ready to assist her, but his shaky voice betrayed him.

"It's okay to be nervous." Lexi reached over and squeezed Billy's arm. "I'm nervous and this isn't my first time in this situation."

"Can I stay, too?" Hunter chewed on his bottom lip, awaiting a response.

Lexi nodded and they walked down the long corridor to the foal's stall. The barn was exceptionally quiet and Lexi eerily felt everyone's eyes were on her. She wasn't a miracle worker and she hated that everyone thought she held the power to keep this horse alive. Nothing was more out of her hands and she had to let nature take its course.

Shane sat in the corner of the stall, the foal standing in front of him, acting essentially normal. This was a better sign than a half hour ago, when it was lying on the floor. Shane rubbed his forehead. Just like his father, the wildest Langtry boy would give his life to save that of a horse. When they were kids, she always found him in the stables or riding one of the many trails. Lexi would be willing to bet his horses held as many of his secrets as her own did.

Directing her attention to the crowd in the hallway, she said, "I think it's best for everyone to go back to bed, and if anything changes, we'll let you know."

Kay agreed and ushered everyone from the barn, leaving Lexi and the three males to stay with the foal.

"Billy, come help me for a minute." Lexi placed the headlight over her hair and turned it on. "I thought I saw a pattern in the coat earlier—almost a cream color on white, but it could have been bedding dust from the pellets."

Lexi attempted to run her hand over the foal's coat. Clearly feeling better, it bounced around the stable. She hoped this wasn't a false sign. When she'd interned in New York, she'd witnessed a perfectly healthy, happy, nursing foal that was predominately white but had some darker markings suddenly turn, and within hours it had to be euthanized. An unsuspecting lethal white, and it wasn't even a pure white horse. Mother Nature was the cruelest and most unpredictable force in the world.

Billy agreed he saw some variations in the horse's shading, making them more optimistic. Hunter curled up on a hay bale near the stall door. Lexi watched him sleep, thinking about the thousands of sleeps she'd missed with him.

She looked over at Shane, who was sitting in the corner of the stall, worry and anguish across his face while he watched the foal's every move. Billy sat in the opposite corner, half-awake. She lowered herself down next to Shane, their shoulders and arms lightly touching. Lexi wanted to comfort and protect him, as she wanted to protect Hunter from the pain they might all feel shortly if the horse didn't make it.

Without hesitation, Shane lifted his arm and wrapped it around Lexi's shoulder, allowing her to settle against his chest. Inhaling his scent of hay and horse, Lexi almost laughed at the irony of him trying to protect her. There were no words between them, no fleeting looks, just a silent understanding and a common hope.

HOLDING LEXI TEMPORARILY erased the pain of the past. He'd forgotten how much he needed her until he felt her body next to him again. Hating to see any animal suffer, Shane wished there was more he could do to help the foal. There was some comfort knowing Lexi had done everything possible, but now they had to watch the clock painfully tick by.

Shane smiled when Hunter shifted in his sleep. All the kids had grown on him, something he never thought possible. Looking down at Lexi, he wondered if they had a chance of having children someday.

"I saw Dylan last night in Belle Fourche." Shane wasn't sure if Lexi wanted to hear about the child that tore them apart but he needed to let her know that chapter of his life was finally closed.

Lexi stiffened slightly before she spoke. "You finally found him after all these years. How did it go?"

"Tab told me Dylan didn't remember me." Shane sighed and rested his head against Lexi's. "He has a brother and a sister, a new mom and what looked like a really nice family."

"You're okay with that?" Lexi asked. "With letting go of him?"

Shane laughed. "What choice do I have? I've wanted to see the kid for the longest time, and when I did, he didn't have a clue who I was. In the back of my mind, I knew he wouldn't. Of course, I hoped he would, but it's better this way. He's happy and that's what really matters."

"Sometimes they're better without us," Lexi said.

"Us?" Shane asked.

Lexi sat up, rolling her shoulders. "It's just a figure of speech. I was generalizing."

Shane felt there was more to it than that but he also knew not to push Lexi. He enjoyed her presence around the ranch and he didn't want to push his luck, although the kiss the other day probably didn't help. Hunter woke and groggily made his way over to them. The foal was curious and sniffed at him. Ramrod-still, Hunter allowed the horse to take inventory before it was seemingly satisfied and walked away.

Weary, Hunter sat down next to Lexi and rested his head against hers. Shane saw Lexi's face go from pink to pale in under a second, her hand frozen in midair as if she didn't know what to do.

"He doesn't bite, Lexi," Shane whispered, trying to recall if he'd seen her with kids before. When the schools did their "visit a profession" day, usually Ashleigh led the groups around and had the most contact with the kids. Lexi gave her speech and that was it.

The foal bounced across the stall, trying out his newly discovered legs, stopping only to urinate, and even then, it was a bouncy event. A few minutes later, he attempted to lie down, bending his front knees and then standing back up, uncertain of the process. Finally finding his coordination, the foal gracefully lowered himself to the ground. Shane saw Lexi place her hand over Hunter's and squeeze gently to reassure him this was normal behavior. Shane had seen a foal's awkwardness a thousand times but they hadn't had a horse this unusual before.

"He seems like every other foal I've seen here, except for his color," Billy said from his corner, startling Lexi. She immediately broke contact with Hunter. "Sorry, I didn't want to interrupt you guys, but are you getting any sign one way or another?"

"I'll feel better when he gets back up on his own,"

Lexi told him. "He should only be down for about thirty minutes, give or take."

It had been a few hours since the foal's birth and they anxiously awaited the horse to do its business. It wasn't what Shane called a date by any means, especially with Billy and Hunter as chaperones, but sitting there, on a stall floor in the middle of the night with Lexi, was pure and real. They had their differences, but horses were the one constant between them and Shane thanked his father every day for bringing Lexi home. He wished he had told Joe that while he was still alive instead of always giving his dad a hard time over one thing or another.

Lexi looked at Shane, and he wondered if she could read his thoughts. Half smiling, she gave him her full attention. "All right, tell me more about Dylan."

Shane bit back the sob that almost broke through. The one he'd been holding since the child he'd loved all these years, the child that he'd sworn to protect and take care of the first year of his life, didn't know who he was. That hurt like hell. He appreciated Lexi wanting to hear more, knowing the mention of Dylan was a reminder of his infidelity.

"He was taller than Hunter, but had the same build," Shane said. "Definite resemblance to Tab, but mostly he favors his mother. I'd stare at Dylan in his crib, trying to find even a little part of him that looked like me. Maybe I knew he wasn't mine, but once I held him all bets were off and I loved that kid. God, I miss him."

"Hunter told me the other night that he has a birthday in a few days." Lexi absently rested her hand on Hunter's shoulder. The boy had fallen asleep with his head on her lap. "I'm assuming you're having a little party for him like Dance of Hope did for Josh's birthday." Recovering from a traumatic brain injury, Josh had turned seven last week and the entire ranch was there to celebrate the occasion with him.

"You're welcome to join us," Shane said. "You know kids—thirteen's a big deal. He's officially a teenager."

"Are his parents flying in?" Lexi asked.

"They're coming at the end of the month for Family Day," Shane said. "They sent a package down that I'm holding in the house for him."

"Family Day?"

Shane felt Lexi stiffen and wrapped his arm around her tighter. "Just like when we were in sleepaway camp. Are you all right?"

Lexi nodded, but Shane once again sensed there was more than she let on. At first he'd dismissed her interest in the school, thinking it was a curiosity, but she seemed to be spending more time around the kids lately, and Shane wondered if her biological clock was kicking in. *I'd love to be the one to stop that clock.*

Taking a chance, he threw the words out there. "Do you ever think about having kids?"

Judging by the look on her face, Shane thought she was about to haul off and slug him. The foal moved and quickly leapt to its feet. Billy slid across the wall to Lexi, causing Hunter to stir awake. Lexi reached out and they all joined hands, anxiously awaiting its next move, all wishing for the same thing. The four of them huddled in the corner of the stall, one white foal staring back at them.

"You should name him Apollo," Hunter whispered.

"Apollo?" He hadn't considered that name before. Regardless of which way this went, the animal deserved to have a name.

"I learned about him in mythology. He was the Greek god of the sun and light and you can't get any lighter than that."

They all laughed. "No, you can't."

The horse moved to the center of the stall and stood still, its tail raised in the air. Shane shut his eyes and said a prayer under his breath. Lexi tightened her grip on his hand.

And there it was. The dark, tarlike meconium that accumulated when the horse fed in the womb. It was the sign they were waiting for.

"Oh, that's gross." Hunter stood and covered his nose.

"That is the most beautiful thing in the world right now." Lexi rose and dusted off her jeans.

"Almost the most beautiful." Shane pulled Lexi in for a hug. "Thank you for being here," he whispered against her hair.

"I'm just doing what you pay me to do." Lexi pulled back, looking him in the eyes.

The tension between them gone, Shane brushed an errant lock of hair out of her face. The feel of her body next to him, touching him, confirmed what he'd known all along. He loved the woman standing before him and no amount of time in the world would change that.

"Are you two going to kiss?" Hunter asked, breaking the moment.

"Come on, kid." Billy ushered him out of the stall. "Let's get some fresh bedding for—are you going to name him Apollo?"

Shane reluctantly stepped away from Lexi, leaving her obviously flustered and blushing.

"I think Apollo's a perfect name," he said.

Hunter smiled and left them alone.

"What do you think, doc?"

"I think we have a dominant white but I'm still going to run a homozygous test for a genetic abnormality. And I'm definitely going to have both parents' stables run further testing—"

Shane placed a finger on her lips to silence her. Closing her eyes, she lowered her head before he had a chance to kiss her.

"Shane." Her voice was barely a whisper. "We can't."

"We can if you let it happen." His breath was warm against her cheek.

SHE WANTED IT TO HAPPEN. She enjoyed the way his arms felt around her body. She missed his scent and most of all she missed his taste.

Reaching up toward him, Lexi laced her fingers behind his neck and drew him in for a kiss. Their tongues met with the sensual familiarity of two longtime lovers. Maybe it was because she'd spent the last few hours with Shane and Hunter. A secret family that no one knew about and a dream fulfilled she'd never thought possible. This was theirs, this was the life she'd wanted all along—the one she deserved. This was—wrong.

Lexi broke their kiss and pushed Shane away. Breathlessly they stared at each other.

"What the hell was that? I think we're getting closer and you pull away again. I can't keep doing this, Lexi."

"Uh-oh," Hunter said from the stall door. "Trouble."

Lexi saw half the ranch standing in the hallway watching their exchange.

"I'm sorry," Billy said. "I thought everyone would want to know the good news."

Flustered, Lexi inhaled sharply. "It's okay." She

walked to the stall door, not daring a glance back. "We need to clean this stall and I want to try nursing again. If we can't then I'll try another mare. Some of the foals are weaning so we should be fine."

"Ashleigh's on her way in." Billy moved aside to let her pass. Shane made no move to follow.

"Thank you." Lexi squeezed Billy's arm and looked down at Hunter, who stood next to him. This time next year he'd probably be taller than she was. Such a strong man in the making. "I'm so proud of you both. That was pretty intense in there and you held up great."

"Thanks." Hunter smiled at her—the pain tugging at her heart almost unbearable. She wanted—she needed—to hug the child she thought was her son and show him how much she loved him.

And his father, too.

Chapter Eight

Lexi swung the stable doors wide with such force she was surprised they remained on their hinges. Thick middle-of-the-night, humidity-laden air made it even harder for her to breathe. She needed to know for certain that was her son who had fallen asleep on her lap. And Shane had kissed her. Why was this happening now?

Knowing she couldn't let this go any further, she had to finish up tonight and keep her distance, even if it meant leaving town until Hunter returned to Colorado. Lexi had a standby large-animal veterinarian she referred people to if she wasn't available. She had faith he'd be able to cover her emergencies.

Steadying herself, she headed back into the stables and peeked at Apollo. He stood there, looking at all the people staring at him as if to say, "What's the big deal?"

"Come on, guys." Chase rounded up his students and led them toward the door. "Time for bed…again."

"Would you like some coffee, dear?" Kay asked while soothingly rubbing Lexi's back. "You look exhausted."

"I would, but I have appointments I need to keep today." Lexi wanted to find Ashleigh and give her a list of things to handle in the morning.

"Take a break and come upstairs with me," Kay gently

demanded. "I'm not taking no for an answer. You look like you're ready to collapse."

Left with no choice and in desperate need of a mini-break, Lexi followed Kay toward the office stairs in the center of the stables.

"If you didn't still have work to do I'd pour you a brandy," Kay whispered from the step above her. "A kiss like that warrants a drink."

No sense wondering if anyone saw them anymore. Soon, the entire town would be chattering about her and Shane's kiss. At least it would take people's minds off the supposed one-nighter she had with Clay.

Upstairs, away from the commotion below, Kay fixed Lexi a cup of coffee and motioned for her to take a seat. The office sat above the stables, with Craftsman-style windows encircling the room, allowing for a 360-degree view. In the moonlight, the ranch had a fairy-tale luminescence to it. In a way, her fairy tale did come true tonight, if only for a little while. The family Lexi thought she'd never have was hers for a few fleeting hours. Then like most dreams, she awoke and it was over.

"Get your bearings about you and then you can get back to work." Kay mothered her like one of her own. She was a kindhearted, hardworking woman who had a grandson a few feet away and Lexi didn't have the guts to tell her the truth.

Lexi rubbed her eyes with the heels of her hands, trying to find relief from the hay dust irritating them. "A part of me could curl up and sleep for hours, the other part is too full of adrenaline."

"It's been a long night," Kay said. "Did something happen before you got here? You seemed upset when you came in."

"No," Lexi said. "I was just going to bed when the phone rang." More like she was going to cry herself to sleep like she had so many other nights.

"When are you going to tell him the truth?"

Knocking her coffee onto the floor, Lexi cursed under her breath. *How does she know?*

"This is exactly what I mean." Kay handed her a roll of paper towels. "You're overly tired, clumsy and you're obviously still in love with my son."

"Wh-what?"

"He hasn't stopped loving you and he does every foolhardy thing there is to forget you, only he knows he can't. We all see it. Why can't you both admit it to each other and get on with it?"

"It's complicated." Lexi wiped up the floor and tried to remain calm. *She doesn't know.*

"Because you both make it complicated," Kay said. "Far be it from me to interfere, but let me say this…you two have wasted so much precious time sidestepping each other it's like watching the world's longest waltz."

Lexi laughed at the picture she painted. "I love you, Kay. Thank you for the coffee, or what I had of it, but I need to finish up down there before my next appointment."

After Ashleigh told her that Crystal still wouldn't allow Apollo to nurse, they brought in Delilah as a surrogate mother. Delilah's foal had completely weaned a day ago and the mare was still producing milk. Apollo instantly took to her and Lexi felt better about the foal getting the proper nutrients.

Placing Apollo and Delilah in an adjacent stall to Crystal's, Lexi hoped Crystal's attitude toward her baby would change. In the meantime, she'd treat both mares as if they were nursing, increasing the food and nutrient intakes.

Before leaving the ranch, Lexi gave Crystal a thorough postfoal exam and then checked on Apollo one last time to ensure he was in fact a normal, healthy foal. Standing alongside his surrogate mom, the white foal looked up at Lexi with his blue eyes, not a care in the world.

Oh, to be a horse.

Lexi sent Ashleigh and Billy home for a few hours, then managed to leave herself without running into Shane again. She was barely able to keep her eyes open when she pulled into her driveway. Resting her head against the steering wheel, she willed herself the strength to get out of the car.

Please let tonight be a dream.

SHANE WALKED WITH Hunter to the bunkhouse, downright confused after that kiss. It was as unexpected as it was natural, and it was perfect until Lexi pushed him away.

"You really like Trouble, don't you?" Hunter asked.

Shane laughed. "What did I tell you about calling her that?"

"Hey, I'm just repeating what you told me the day I met her." They stopped on the bunkhouse steps. "I'm not tired and the sun's going to be up in a few anyway. Do I have to go back to bed?"

The sky to the east showed a hint of light gray and the stars were beginning to fade. The evening crickets had long since tucked up their legs and called it a night while the birds had begun their morning song.

"The Magpie opens in a bit. Think you can manage

to quietly grab some clothes from inside?" Shane looked down at Hunter's bare feet. "And boots?"

Hunter snuck into the dark bunkhouse. It reminded him of when Shane and his brothers were kids and Jesse would sneak into the bunkhouse trying to steal the ranch hands' boots. Jesse was always the prankster, and Shane was surprised his brother didn't get himself shot with half his shenanigans. He missed those days, when life wasn't so complicated.

Minutes later, Hunter eased the door closed and they headed up to the main house. Barely containing his amazement, Hunter walked into the Langtrys' kitchen overlooking the great room.

"Wow!" The moon shone through the large sky-light, highlighting the rustic log walls. Shane's father had taken great care choosing hand-hewn beams in-stead of machined lumber. His mother's respect for the local Native American Kickapoo tribe was evident in the beaded artwork that adorned the walls. But Shane's favorite part of the house was always the monumental, floor-to-ceiling river-rock fireplace.

"Come on." Shane led the way up the stairs to the loft, making the room below appear even grander. "You can shower down the hall and I'll meet you out here in a few."

Unable to tear himself away from the railing, Hunter looked around the golden-timbered space. "This is even bigger than the lodge my family goes to in Aspen. You must be mega-rich."

Shane grinned at the boy's innocence. Most days he forgot how privileged he'd had it growing up. He didn't know much about Hunter's parents, aside from rodeo, and even then, they seemed a little out of their element.

They were more the nine-to-five desk-job type, whose idea of a vacation was a spa retreat instead of a camping trip.

"Take your shower so we can eat and be back before the rest of your class wakes up."

The cold shower did nothing to quell his thoughts of Lexi. The same passion had still coursed through their bodies when they'd kissed. Shane thought it would feel like it used to, but instead there'd been something unfamiliar and much more personal than in any kiss they'd ever shared before. Longing and need coupled with a raw and complete devotion he couldn't explain. He needed to have her back in his arms, his bed and his life because tonight confirmed it—she'd never left his heart.

"Lexi!" A LOUD banging surrounded her. She tried to move and her back ached like hell. "Lexi, open the damn door before I rip the roof off."

"Daddy?" Lexi opened her eyes. She was still in her car, in the driveway, and her father was pounding on the side window. Reaching for the door, she flicked the power lock button.

"Are you sick?" Jim Lawson pulled her from the car. "I heard you pull in but when you didn't get out of the car I began to wonder."

"I'm just tired," Lexi said. "I had a long night."

"You better not be drunk." Jim turned her to look at him. "Are you?"

Lexi shrugged out of his grasp. "I haven't come home drunk since I was in college."

"Where were you all night?"

"The fifth degree, Dad? Really?" Lexi trudged to the

side door of the house, leaving her boots in the mud-room. "You know I'm on call twenty-four hours a day."

"I'm usually asleep when you're on call." Her dad harrumphed and sat down at the small table against the kitchen wall. "Was it an emergency or a foal?"

"Both." Lexi opened the refrigerator and grabbed a can of Diet Coke, popping the top. "What on earth are you wearing?"

Jim's tattered, flannel bathrobe, which he refused to throw out, barely covered his bright blue, cartoon-cow boxers and a white, sleeveless undershirt.

"I was worried." Jim looked down at the stain on his shirt and scratched at it. "Hmm, wonder where that came from."

"I'm fine, and I'll tell you about it after I clean up and get into some fresh clothes." She checked her watch. "I suggest you do the same. I guess it's morning anyway."

In the safety of the bathroom, Lexi locked the door and took a quick shower. She didn't want to stop moving and she certainly didn't want to think. People and animals relied on her and there was no room for emotion in her work.

Lexi went out to check on her own horses before she left, when someone cleared their throat at the other end of the barn.

"Hello?" Lexi called out.

"Heard you had quite a night." Clay strode to the stall door.

"Sure did. Got to spend most of it in extremely close quarters with Hunter." Lexi wiped at her eyes, and grabbed a rubber curry comb from the shelf. Grooming Autumn calmed her nerves and the horse loved the attention. "I'm assuming you're here because you have the test results."

"He's your son, Lexi."

Lexi froze midstroke, bracing herself against Autumn. "Thank you. Let me know how much I owe you for everything."

Clay unlatched the stall door, but didn't open it. "Come out here, Lex, so we can talk."

Ignoring him, she continued her circular motions on the horse's body.

"And his family?"

"Lexi?" Clay hesitated. "I wish you'd—"

"And his family?" Lexi said through gritted teeth.

"Soccer mom, business dad, no debts, no criminal charges, not even a speeding ticket. You chose a good family, Lexi, and you did right by your son. Don't beat yourself up over this."

"I'll be fine." Lexi placed the comb on the shelf and walked out of the stall. "It's not like I didn't already know it. I just need a few minutes to let it sink in then I have to get back to work."

"Not until I make sure you're all right. When was the last time you ate?"

"Yesterday at the picnic, I guess." Food was the last thing on her mind.

"Well, I certainly didn't see you eat and you left early. Come on, we're getting breakfast. We don't have to talk but I'm not leaving you like this and that's final."

"Fine." Lexi didn't want to argue, she didn't want to think, either. The more she thought, the more she felt. She just wanted to work and keep her mind occupied. There was always safety in keeping busy. "My car... I'll drive."

"Considering the front seat of my truck is loaded with crap we have no other choice, but Lexi, I'm driving."

Being a passenger in her own car felt foreign to her. At least when she drove she had control, and right now her life was spinning out of control.

"Hunter's parents are coming to town for Family Day at the end of the month and I don't know how to handle it."

Clay pulled the car off to the side of the road and faced Lexi. "You need to decide once and for all if you're really going to keep this from Shane and Hunter. I know you said there's no point in telling them, but you need to look at this from all angles."

"Meaning if they found out later on." Lexi knew the obvious answer was to come clean to everyone and let the chips fall where they may. The logical side of her reasoned that what they didn't know couldn't hurt them, and if their relationship were only a temporary one, she might be able to get away with it. Shane had already traveled to a few of Hunter's events and Lexi was certain there were more to come. If their resemblance increased, someone was bound to ask questions. With Shane's wild history, a paternity test wouldn't be that far off-base, but once you did the math, she was the only possibility as Hunter's mother.

"Are you prepared to keep this secret from Shane forever?" Clay asked. "You two have gotten closer recently. Can you live with this?"

"I've lived with it all these years." Lexi shrugged. "This isn't much different."

"It's a lot different, Lex. You didn't know where or who he was. Now you do and he has an ongoing relationship with his father."

Lexi laid her head against the car seat and closed her eyes. "I have to do what's best for Hunter and that would be not to disrupt his life. I can handle the guilt and the pain. I've been handling it all along. No one needs or deserves to get hurt, Clay. We need to let it rest."

The conversation over, Clay continued to drive to the Magpie. Lexi agreed to a quick bite and then she'd start her rounds. She needed to call Ashleigh and have her keep an eye on the horses at Bridle Dance. Determined to keep her distance this time, Lexi wasn't taking any more chances around Hunter and Shane. She knew the truth. She'd made her decision years ago and that was that. Nothing was going to change.

"Isn't that her car?" Hunter asked when they parked in front of the Magpie. "I thought horse vets drove trucks."

"She has a Ram 3500 Dually she uses for trailering horses," Shane said. "But it's easier and cheaper to use her car for typical ranch calls."

Lexi's mud-covered Mustang sat in front of the luncheonette, in desperate need of a wash and wax. Clay had told him to surprise her if he wanted to win her back, and he knew Lexi definitely wasn't the traditional-gift type. Shane tried to think of a way he could get her car detailed without her knowledge. In high school, she'd stolen his filthy white pickup and detailed it when he was away at a weekend rodeo. When he returned he didn't even recognize the truck was his. It was a sweet gesture he'd never had the chance to return.

"How are you at stealing cars?" Shane asked.

Hunter's head shot up. "We're going to steal her car?"

"In a manner of speaking and I need your help."

Shane told Hunter his plan, but they needed a way

to see it through. Figuring she'd be at the ranch later, they decided that if Hunter kept her occupied, Shane would have a golden opportunity, with a limited amount of time.

Bells above the door jingled as they entered the cozy luncheonette. The handful of Formica-and-chrome tables were already filled to capacity but one booth was still empty—right behind Lexi's spot at the counter. Nerves began to hitch a ride to his palms and he wiped the sweat on his jeans. A seasoned pro at women, Shane knew his typical charm was out of the question.

Hunter nudged him. "Just say hi," he whispered. "Keep it simple."

Shane looked down at the kid in annoyance. "Oh, okay, coach." His sarcasm was thick.

"It's better than standing here," Hunter retorted. "Just sayin'."

Shane tapped Lexi on the shoulder. "Hi." The word came out slow, mumbled like he had a mouthful of marbles. Hunter rolled his eyes and squeezed in on the other side of Lexi, almost causing her to fly off the stool.

Great team we make, kid.

"What are you two doing here?" Lexi's eyes darted from one to the other. "Don't the students eat at the ranch?"

The harshness of her tone made Hunter retreat toward the booth. He sat down and removed a menu from behind the napkin holder, ignoring them. Either he was giving them a moment to talk or she'd hurt his feelings. Shane was pissed.

"Attitude check?" Shane said to Lexi. "You want to be mad at me for a kiss? Fine, but don't take it out on him."

Lexi looked around the luncheonette, checking to

see if the other customers had overheard. Their immediate downward glances confirmed they had and Lexi laid her fork on her empty plate and stood. Leaving a twenty on the counter, she walked out the door, leaving him to stand in the middle of the Magpie with his hat in his hand.

Clay strode from the bathroom and motioned toward the counter. "Hey, man, where'd she run off to?"

"She just left," Shane said. "Did you two come together?"

He knew there was a rumor going around town about Clay and Lexi, and naturally he blew it off. But seeing them together in the morning made him wonder.

"We did but it's not what you think. Nash is taking a look at my truck and Lexi and I decided to grab a bite to eat while I waited. I'd better catch up to her before she leaves me here. I'll call you later."

Shane slid into the booth across from Hunter. "I'm sorry she treated you that way. She was out of line."

"Forget about it. What the hell was that *hhhiii* business?" Hunter set his menu on the table and stared at him. "Did someone set your mouth on hot and it ran?"

"Watch your tone, and that's what you told me to say." The little man had a set. Shane opened his menu, although he knew the thing by heart. "What do you want to order?"

"I didn't tell you to say it like that." Hunter reached across the table and pulled Shane's menu down. "It sounded like you had a mouthful of molasses."

"You're going to give me advice on women?" Shane laughed.

"Yeah, I think I should," Hunter asserted. "I do pretty well myself at home."

"Oh, you do?"

"Running off my customers so early in the morning?" Bridgett stood at their table with her short pink uniform and white apron. "What can I get you two?"

Hunter mouthed "watch this" to Shane and turned his body toward the waitress.

"Your hair reminds me of a warm summer day at sunset."

Oh, no, he didn't. Bridgett smiled, color rising to her cheeks. "Aren't you just the sweetest thing. Do you like pancakes, because we make the best chocolate chip pancakes in the world."

"I'd love some." Hunter beamed, clearly proud of himself.

"And you?" Bridgett asked Shane with far less enthusiasm, almost bordering on disdain. "Your typical—I mean your usual?"

Shane nodded and Hunter almost fell out of the booth laughing at him. "She likes me better than you," he mocked.

"I have to admit, that was a good pickup line." Shane laughed. "I guess I did ruffle a few feathers this morning."

"We only talked to two women this morning and they're both mad at you." Hunter looked toward Bridgett and waved. "What's the deal with the redhead? Why does she hate you?"

"Bridgett happens to be Lexi's best friend. So if Lexi is ticked at me, so's Bridgett."

"Nah, I'll soften her up for you," Hunter said. "Are you going to let me have a cup of coffee or are you going to tell me it will stunt my growth like my parents do?"

"Go right ahead." Shane couldn't remember ever not drinking coffee. "You'll need it today."

"I hear we have a little heartbreaker in our midst." Maggie Dalton turned their cups over and filled them both with coffee.

"Maggie…" Shane began before Hunter could work his charms on the woman. "This is Hunter Rathbone, one of my students. Hunter, this is Cole's wife Tess's mother, Maggie."

"It's a real pleasure to meet you, ma'am." Hunter grinned innocently. "I can see why Tess is so beautiful."

Not again.

"Aren't you cuter than a kitten in pajamas!" Maggie turned to Shane. "He reminds me of you when you were that age."

"Thanks." Shane smiled. *At least someone noticed me.*

"Listen." Maggie leaned into Hunter. "Don't take any advice about women from this one here, trust me."

She winked and walked away.

"You must be some dog." Hunter tugged a napkin out of the dispenser. "The things you can learn from me."

"Oh, that will be the day." Shane smirked.

"What did you do to her anyway? You said something about getting married the other day."

"I was supposed to marry Lexi and ended up marrying someone else."

"Knocked a chick up, huh?"

Shane almost choked on his coffee. "Precocious, aren't you? And yes and no. The kid turned out not to be mine."

"Gold digger or just a tramp?" Hunter said so matter-of-factly Shane didn't believe he was talking to a kid.

"Both, and you ask too many questions."

"Do you want my help with Lexi or not?" Hunter asked. "At the rate you're going, every female in town will be throwing eggs at you by sundown."

"Here you go, honey." Bridgett set Hunter's pancakes down in front of him, complete with a giant whipped cream heart on top of them. She gave Shane his order without a word and walked away.

"All right, you win. I need your help."

Chapter Nine

"Where are you off to in a hurry?" Clay tried to stop Lexi from leaving without him

"Hop in and I'll drop you off at your truck." Lexi stepped on the gas before Clay even closed the door. "I appreciate your help, but it's over with now. I'm taking your advice and steering clear of them. While they're eating it gives me a chance to check in at the ranch and head out before they return."

"My advice was *before* you found out, not after." Clay held on to the dashboard while Lexi turned off Main Street. "Follow your heart, Lexi, but try not to kill us in the process."

"No, absolutely not." Following her heart was selfish. "This isn't about what I want. I take that back... yes, it is. I want Hunter to be healthy and happy and he is. He doesn't need to know I'm his biological mother."

Minutes later they were in her driveway, behind his truck. Clay stepped from the Mustang and before he could say another word, Lexi threw the car in Reverse and left Clay with no other option than to close the door and let her leave. Her feelings weren't important and she'd known that the day she decided to bring a child into this world. Giving him up for adoption was painful, but the more Lexi thought about it, it wasn't the most painful thing in the world. Seeing hurt and distrust on Hunter's face would be, and she wouldn't be able to live with that.

At the ranch, Apollo and Crystal both checked out perfectly. Ashleigh had tried unsuccessfully once again to introduce mother and baby without any luck. Not willing to push the matter any further, Lexi resolved that Delilah would be Apollo's new mother since they appeared to be forming a bond. The animal world and human world weren't that different after all.

By the time she finished on the ranch, Shane and Hunter were driving in, passing her on the main road. She didn't wave and she didn't even look in their direction. Keeping her eyes straight ahead, Lexi gripped the wheel and headed home.

It was later than usual for Autumn's morning ride, but Lexi would rather go out late than miss their alone time. Opting to ride bareback today, she directed Autumn to the trail behind the crops. Nowhere near the size of Bridle Dance, the Lawson farm had a modest amount of acreage and enough land to ride multiple trails and not get bored.

The reins loose in her hand, Lexi allowed Autumn to choose their destination. Figuring the horse would pick her favorite spot near the small fishing pond, they instead made their way toward the north end of Cooter Creek, where it first entered Ramblewood. Autumn languidly walked along the water's edge and Lexi knew her horse sensed her tension and was allowing her the time to unwind.

Horses amazed her the way they noticed your every emotion. It was one of the reasons she loved to ride without a saddle. She felt more connected with the animal and she trusted Autumn completely.

Taking longer than expected, she called from the trail to check in with Ashleigh. The Lawsons' market and gift shop had a separate back area with its own outside entrance that Lexi had converted into her office. She needed to send out some invoices and check her patient vaccination schedules. They would have to get a start on the next round of West Nile within the coming week.

"Hello?" Ashleigh said.

"It's me. Are you in the office yet?"

"I'm here with Billy and Michelle starting the West Nile and influenza schedule."

Michelle was one of their summer techs home from college. She was two years away from her bachelor's then she was off to veterinary school. Once again, Lexi's techs were one step ahead of her.

"Well, that takes care of the reason I was calling." Lexi lifted her face toward the sun. "I'm out on Autumn but I'll be in before my next appointment."

She had a follow-up with a show jumper in the afternoon, leaving her with the rest of the morning for herself. Lexi hopped off and led Autumn to the water to drink. When she was finished, Lexi wound her arms around the mare's neck, and Autumn lifted her front leg and wrapped it around Lexi's waist. It was a trick Jesse trained his horses to do, and one she taught Autumn when she was a yearling.

Thinking about Jesse made her wonder about Miranda. When she'd left the picnic the poor woman looked like she was about to pop. She wasn't due for another three weeks but the doctor told her it could be sooner, especially when carrying twins.

There it was…once again she was thinking about Hunter. Placing both hands on Autumn's back, she hopped and swung her leg over.

Maybe it's time I moved on from Ramblewood.

SHANE HADN'T SEEN Lexi in three days and there was no doubt in his mind she was avoiding him. She came in early the first day, so he thought he'd catch her on the second. That morning she sent Ashleigh instead and showed up when he was teaching class. Thinking he'd outsmart her, today he held class outside since a slight cool front had come through, but she didn't show at all.

He called Clay before the afternoon class began and asked if he'd heard from her.

"I haven't seen her, either," Clay said. "Have you tried her office or her house?"

"Every time I step foot on their land one of her kin threatens to shoot me," Shane groaned. "I'm not exactly the Lawsons' favorite person."

"Give her some time, she'll come around."

"Time for what?" Shane pinched the bridge of his nose. "Do you know something you're not telling me?"

"You've been a little pushy lately," Clay laughed. "You went from patiently waiting for her to let you back in to shoving your tongue down her throat in the middle of the stables."

"I'll have you know she kissed me," Shane said indignantly.

"I'm talking about last week, not the other day."

"How the hell do you know about that?" Shane demanded.

"You kissed her in a public place," Clay said. "Do

you realize how many employees you have working for you? People talk, man."

"Will you call her for me?" Shane hated to ask his friend to get in the middle of things, but Lexi wasn't making the situation easy and he wasn't going to give up on her.

"I can try. Any particular message you want me to tell her? Maybe three little words?"

"Don't you dare," Shane threatened. "Just, I don't know, have her call me and mention Hunter's birthday party. She knows about it, but she may have forgotten."

Shane pocketed his phone and headed toward the arena.

"Any luck?" Chase called out when he opened the gate.

"Clay's going to try to reach her." Shane double-checked some of the rigging hanging on the rails. "I'm supposed to ride in Tennessee this week."

"You going to go?" Chase removed one of the hack reins for a closer inspection.

"I should." Shane exhaled slowly. "I hate leaving this all on you."

"No bother." Chase smiled, placed the rein back on the fence and continued on to the saddle rigging. "I'm not going to think twice when I do it to you next month. Don't blame not going on the rodeo school, Shane. If you want to stay because of whatever is going on between you and Lexi, then stay and tell her why you're staying."

"I would if she'd talk to me." Shane adjusted his chaps and the class started to file in.

"If it were me, I'd go to Tennessee for a chance to clear your head," Chase said. "It's two days, it's not like she's going anywhere. All right, class, let's—"

"Shane! Chase!" His mother screamed across the parking lot. "They're coming!"

Hopping the fence, Shane grabbed his mother before she fainted. "Calm down. Who's coming?"

"The babies!" She fanned her face. "We have to go."

"You're not driving anywhere." Chase ushered his mom toward the door. "Are Miranda and Jesse at the hospital?"

"On their way." Kay's voice was ragged. "You drive then."

"You coming?" Chase called over his shoulder.

"Kyle, you got this?" Shane asked.

"I'm good. Just go." Kyle waved him out. "Give them my best."

"I'm not going in that doorless thing," Kay said as she pointed at Shane's Jeep.

"We're taking your car, Mom." Chase held the door open for her before she pushed it closed.

"Not like that you aren't. You're not getting my Mercedes dirty—go get changed."

"I thought you wanted to leave now?" Shane asked.

"No sons of mine are going to the hospital with dirt on their faces and heaven only knows what under their nails."

"We've certainly gone looking worse." Shane nudged Chase.

"I meant the maternity ward. Oh, shit." Kay fumbled for her phone. "I forgot to call Tess. Where's Cole?"

Shane and Chase laughed at their mother's infrequent swearword and scrambled into the house to make themselves more hospital presentable. By the time they arrived, the rest of the family was in the waiting room along with Mable and Lexi.

"I'm just glad we got her here before she birthed those babies on my clean floor," Mable said.

Animated as usual, the woman filled in everyone who entered the immediate vicinity. Strangers and all. "Can you imagine the handful these young'uns are going to be with those two as parents? Stubborn, I'll tell you that much. I just wish I knew what they were."

"We all do," Kay said. "I'm so tired of knitting yellow or green. Leave it to them to make it difficult on us and wait until they're born to find out the sex."

Shane wrinkled his nose at the antiseptic smell of the hospital. He crossed the room toward Lexi, and she squared her shoulders as he drew near. He wondered if she'd bolt at any second.

"I get the distinct impression you've been avoiding me." Shane sat in the chair next to her.

Lexi loudly sighed and slumped in the chair. "I've had quarterly West Nile vaccines to administer around the county, plus six-month influenza for all the yearlings." She rose to leave and Shane grabbed her hand. Her fingers were cold and stiff, like icicles.

"Please don't go," Shane implored. "How did you hear about Miranda so fast?"

"I was the driver," Lexi grumbled, lowering herself back down into the chair.

"What?" Shane chuckled. "How did that happen?"

"I was vaccinating Jesse's horses when Miranda went into labor. Can you imagine Mable or Jesse driving here?"

"Please tell me you didn't squeeze them all in your Mustang." Shane didn't even want to imagine it.

"Didn't I?" Lexi's brows rose. "I had no choice. Mable's car is a scary-ass bucket of bolts and there was no way Miranda was getting her baby belly up and into a truck. They seriously need to rethink the vehicle situation over there. So, Miranda rode up front with me and I squeezed Mable and Jesse in the back."

Shane laughed. "Was the top up, at least?"

"Heavens, no." Lexi started to laugh. "There is no way Jesse would fit in that backseat if it was."

"Mable must have loved that."

"That woman screamed the entire way here like a damn police siren." Tears trailed down Lexi's face. "Believe me when I tell you, they heard us coming."

Shane howled. "My poor brother."

"My poor ears! Miranda was the easiest one of the bunch and she was in labor."

Shane swiped his eyes with the back of his hand. "I think you deserve a medal."

"Screw that," Lexi said. "I want a trophy."

It felt good to laugh, especially with Lexi. The tension was gone, at least for a few moments while they waited for the next Langtry generation to arrive.

"There's something I've wanted to tell you for a few days now," Shane began.

"Should I be worried?" Lexi said. "You're not pregnant, are you?"

Shane bit his bottom lip, not sure how to respond. "At least we can joke about it."

"It's either laugh or cry and I prefer laughter."

"Well, this will really make you laugh." Shane's excitement rose at the idea of his television show. "I was approached at the ribbon cutting to do a reality show centering on me and the school."

"Someone wants you as their reality?" Lexi giggled. "Now that's funny."

Feeling a bit wounded, Shane didn't respond.

"You're serious?" Lexi asked. "I heard rumblings about it but I thought it was a story one of the local news stations was running on the school. I'm sorry— continue."

"They're choosing a few rodeo cowboys and shooting the segments all over the country. Of course, they want us to meet up at the same rodeo events so we can have on-screen time together, but they want me and Ride 'em High! as the show's anchor."

"What about Chase?" Lexi asked. "The school is half his."

"It's all still up in the air and we haven't had a chance to sit down with anyone from the show yet." Even though he and Chase hadn't agreed to do the show, they still wanted to send a production crew out to look around. "They want to take some test shots this week, but if we do go through with it, they'll probably ask you to sign a waiver of some sort."

"Me?" Lexi asked. "How do I fit into all of this?"

"Everyone does. They'll film in and around the ranch, plus in town. I'll have a camera crew following me."

"Count me out, cowboy." Lexi shook her head. "I don't want any part of that."

"Now you sound like my mom and Cole."

"Keep them the hell away from me, Shane." Lexi stood and walked outside before he could stop her.

"Please answer, please answer, please answer." Lexi spoke into the phone while she paced in front of the hospital.

"You've reached CT Investigations. I'm unavailable

at this time. Please leave a message and I'll return your call shortly."

"It's Lexi. I need to talk to you right away. It's urgent."

"So start talking." Clay appeared between two parked cars.

"Don't do that!"

"I told you I can get in and out undetected," Clay joked. "Is everything okay with the babies?"

"Everything's fine." Lexi dragged him away from the hospital entrance. "Did you know someone asked Shane to do a reality show here in Ramblewood?"

"He told me the other day, I tried to talk to you about it but you haven't returned any of my calls." Clay relaxed on a brick parking lot break wall. "You can't be anywhere near that show."

"No kidding!" Lexi began to panic. *This can't be happening.* "But how can I avoid it if they're filming everywhere? Especially if they look into his past, they'll find me."

"When you gave your son up for adoption, did you use your real name in the hospital?" Clay asked.

"Was there another way? Because I wasn't given any options." Lexi wildly threw her arms in the air. "That's bad, isn't it?"

"Who paid your hospital bills?" Clay asked.

"The agency handled everything." Lexi stared at him. "It was part of the adoption."

"And you've checked your credit report to make sure nothing from back then has shown up? Nothing was past due or went into collections?"

"No, but that was almost thirteen years ago." Lexi

dismissed the idea. "Even if there was, they'd have dropped off my credit report after seven years."

"Not if the account was sold." Clay had her attention and realization started to set in. "Each time an account is sold, it goes on your credit report and then it remains for seven years."

"What?" Lexi sat on the wall next to Clay. "How can I get a copy and check?"

"Normally you would check these things every year online but I'll do it and I'll run an extensive background check on you to see if there are any surprises lurking out there. Keep in mind, I'm not the only investigator out there and these shows love to dig up dirt. If someone finds out you went to school out there and combines that with Hunter living in Denver and then you factor in the resemblance thing and your reluctance to be on the show, you'll be in trouble."

"And if they find out..." Lexi didn't need to finish the sentence. She knew she had to tell Shane the truth.

CLAY ENTERED THE waiting area with Lexi close behind.

"Look who I found in the parking lot?" She sat down on the opposite side of the room and nervously bounced her leg up and down.

Clay made his way around the room, asking for the latest update before he took a seat next to Shane.

"What's up with her?" Shane nodded toward Lexi. "Did she tell you she raised Cain over just the thought of being on the show?"

"Are you sure you want to do this thing?" Clay asked. "You're facing some pretty tough opposition. The only people on your side are Chase and your students, and you need to make the parents aware there's a production crew coming, even for test shots of the grounds."

"Not you, too?"

Shane was about to argue when a nurse appeared. "Langtry family?" Everyone said yes in unison. "Both Mommy and babies are doing fine. Daddy not so much."

"What happened to my son?" Kay asked. "All he had to do was stand there!"

"Well, Mr. Langtry had a little problem in that department. It's not unusual, but we stitched him up."

"Stitched?" Shane snickered.

"He hit his head when he passed out," the nurse said.

"Fool child," Mable said. "Can you tell us the sex of the babies?"

"Two boys." The woman smiled. "Congratulations, Grandmas."

"Grandmas?" Mable repeated. "I'm not the babies' grandma."

"On the contrary. Two visitors may go in and Miranda asked for both grandmothers."

"Oh, dearest me." Mable's eyes began to well with tears. "I'm a grandma too, Kay! We're both grandmas!"

Everyone laughed, everyone except Shane. Dylan was born in this very hospital, with the entire family gathered around. He understood why his brother passed out. A birth wasn't something you wanted to watch every day, but you couldn't tear yourself away when it was your own child. The child you helped to create, or at least thought you did.

"How are you doing?" Lexi asked. "I know this must bring back some memories."

"I still can't believe Sharon let me believe Dylan was my son for an entire year. It was cruel."

"Mmm, I was never convinced she knew who the father was," Lexi said. "I think she chose the one with the most money."

"I wish she hadn't and we'd still be together." Shane searched her eyes for some recognition in return.

"It doesn't change the fact that you cheated on me, and honestly, I don't want to rehash that. But we do need to talk."

"We do, and there's something I need to tell you, too, but not here." Shane looked around the waiting room. "Let's grab a cup of coffee."

The only choice in the cafeteria this late was coffee or soda and snack crackers. Sitting across from her, Shane tried to find the nerve to tell Lexi he loved her and that he'd never stopped.

She looked tired and withdrawn and he wondered what she wanted to tell him. There was a nagging feeling in the pit of his stomach that she was about to announce that she and Clay were together, despite both of their denials. Shane didn't want to give her the chance to say the words. She needed to hear how he felt first and maybe...

"Lexi," he began. "I—I want a second chance."

Okay, so it wasn't exactly how he planned it but it was close enough. He'd made a direct declaration of his...of his what? *Attraction?*

"I mean, you and I have a past." *Spit it out already.* "And I think we can have a future together and I—"

"There you are," Clay interrupted. "Your brother's asking for you."

Shane exhaled the words *love you,* under his breath but she didn't hear him. "Which brother?"

"The one that just became a father." Clay looked incredulously at Shane and then at Lexi. "Bad timing?"

His friend just stopped him from making a fool out of himself.

"Nope, you're right on schedule."

"WERE YOU ABOUT to tell him?" Clay asked after Shane left the cafeteria.

"Yes!" Lexi ran a hand through her hair and looked up toward the fluorescent lights. "For a detective, this here—" Lexi waved her fingers around the empty room "—should have been your first clue. Quiet, out-of-the-way place. The two of us alone. Are you picking up what I'm putting down, Magnum?"

"I didn't think you'd do it right now!" Clay huffed.

"Why not?" Lexi stood. "There's no good time."

Lexi returned to the waiting room when Vicki arrived. "We couldn't get a sitter this late so I finally told Brandon to stay home with Randi Lynn and I came on my own. She really had a short labor, huh?"

Lexi had been in labor for twenty-two hours with Hunter. Several epidurals didn't completely kill the pain and she understood why some people wanted to be unconscious. Then there were people like Vicki, who got overexcited at a baby shower and gave birth in a matter of minutes. Easy peasy and call it a day.

"Lexi, you can go in and see her now." Kay ushered Lexi towards the hallway.

"Vicki's here, she can go before me." Lexi knew Shane was still in there and a hospital room with a baby was the last place she wanted to be.

"You go on," Vicki insisted. "You drove her here. You deserve to go in first."

"Room 226 on the left." Kay pointed down the corridor.

The cream-colored walls seemed to close in on Lexi while she trekked down the hallway, painfully taking her time, hoping Shane would appear and return to the waiting area.

Room 226. There it was. Miranda, Jesse and the babies were on the other side of that door. And so was Shane. She inhaled deeply and let out a long slow breath. Knocking lightly, she gingerly pushed the door open and peeked inside.

Jesse opened the door the rest of the way. "They just fell asleep. Come on in."

Lexi tried not to stare at the bandage on his forehead when she hugged her old friend.

"Congratulations," she whispered.

Shane sat in the recliner cradling one of the boys, rocking slowly and staring intently into the infant's face. Lexi was unable to choke back the tears she'd been holding the moment she walked in the room, and let them spill over. Shifting focus, she looked at Miranda holding a tiny wrapped bundle.

"I'm so happy for you." Lexi squeezed her free hand.

"Thank you," Miranda softly said. "This is Jackson and that's Slade."

"They are so precious." Lexi didn't dare gaze in Shane's direction. "I love their names."

"Here," Shane said behind her. "You can hold him. Slade, meet Lexi."

Their bodies touched as Shane placed Slade in her arms. Unable to control herself, she looked into his eyes.

Now she knew. She knew exactly how it would have felt if Shane was there when Hunter was born.

Holding Slade in her arms, she sat down in the chair and cried.

Chapter Ten

After her emotional breakdown at the hospital, Lexi managed to limit her time on the ranch. She was thrilled to hear Shane had gone to Tennessee for a few days, and when he came back, she made herself nonexistent. Despite swearing she'd keep her distance, at the last minute she decided there was no way she'd miss her son's birthday. Shane and Clay had both called that morning to remind her she was invited to the party they'd planned for that afternoon, reassuring Lexi that the reality show had finished taping. This was her first and last birthday with her son and she was determined to enjoy every second of it.

The barbecue pits were located near the bunkhouse and Lexi was glad she wore a pair of old sneakers to walk up the hill. She had her bathing suit on under her shorts and tank top in case everyone decided to go swimming.

Lexi loved the family atmosphere of the ranch birthday parties. Kay knew it was hard for the resident hippotherapy kids to be away from home and friends on their birthdays, so she'd decided to throw a party for each of them when their birthdays rolled around. Shane and

Chase followed suit with Ride 'em High! and between both facilities, this was the second birthday this month.

After a lunch of barbecued hamburgers, hot dogs and corn on the cob, Shane and Chase carried out a huge sheet cake with a cartoon version of Hunter on top of a bucking bareback.

"Tight!" Hunter shouted.

Since it was Sunday and they didn't have classes today, they rode four-wheelers down to the river for a swim. Thanks to Hunter's machinations, Lexi ended up on the back of Shane's ATV and had to hold on to his waist for dear life. He drove the blasted quad the way he drove that Jeep of his, wide open all the way.

It had been years since she'd swung on a rope swing and Lexi wasn't sure she trusted anything that hung from a tree since grade school. "You're up, babe." Shane handed her the rope.

"I don't think so, babe." She didn't need to swing out over the water and lose half of her bathing suit. What possessed her to wear a red bikini to a birthday party anyway? *Because you knew Shane would like it.* But like it or not, she was not taking her tank top off.

As she waded into the water, someone came up behind her and pushed her under. Resurfacing, she looked around to see Hunter laughing hysterically.

"You are asking for it." Lexi splashed water in his direction.

"Uh-huh." Hunter nodded. "But you have to catch me first."

Lexi dived under the water and swam toward him. He may have had the element of surprise but she had speed on her side. Especially since she was on the swim team in high school. Within seconds she was upon him. Grabbing hold of his foot, she tugged him under the water.

Both came up for air at the same time.

"What was that you were saying?" Lexi asked.

"That's not fair." Hunter splashed her. "I didn't know you were that fast."

Lexi laughed. "You're the one who asked for it."

Hunter starting laughing again.

"What's so—" Lexi felt herself rise out of the water and fly through the air. "Shane!"

Lexi jumped on his back and unsuccessfully tried to push him under. Seeing her struggle, Hunter joined her and together they were able to take him down.

"Who said anything about tag teams?" Shane pushed his hair back from his face, water dripping from his nose. "You two cheat and you know what happens to cheaters?"

Shane scooped her up in one arm and Hunter in the other, not letting either of them go. For the moment, Lexi allowed herself to enjoy what a summer day would have been like if she hadn't give her son up for adoption.

"Thank you for coming today," Shane said later as he sat down next to her in one of the Adirondack chairs. "I think this was the most fun we've had together since we were kids celebrating our own birthdays."

"I'm glad I came." Lexi admired the man beside her. "You've changed since you built the school. Do I dare say you're tamer and more enjoyable to be around?"

"I know, it's so strange," Shane agreed. "I thought by the end of each day I'd be champing at the bit to get out of here, but I'm not. I'm actually going to miss these guys when they leave. Spending time with these kids has really made me rethink my life."

"You won't have time to miss them with your next class in August and your reality show." Lexi bit back the bile on that last part.

"The show's not a definite. *Nothing's* definite and my agent's not a fan of the idea. Plus I noticed you weren't thrilled with the idea."

After Clay ran a background check on her and didn't come up with anything linking her to Hunter, she felt more secure, but that didn't mean she was willing to take the chance.

"I told you how I felt about that, Shane. I'm not going to change my mind."

"What about us? Think you can change your mind about that?"

"I think we can discuss it, but I'm not making any promises." Lexi knew she shouldn't lead him on. She knew a relationship was impossible with a secret this deep. And if he did the reality show, there was definitely no way they'd be together, but the word *no* wouldn't come out of her mouth. She wanted another chance at happiness with Shane in spite of it all.

"Do you want to open up the gift your parents sent down?" Shane stood when Hunter walked over to them.

Kay and Lexi joined Shane and Hunter at the picnic table while the teen eagerly tore at the silver gift wrap. Inside, one of a cowboy's favorite items appeared.

"Now I have one just like you." Hunter placed the straw Stetson on his head and tipped it forward slightly to match Shane's.

"That's sharp-looking," Kay said, while Barney tried to squirm out of her arms. "You can even wear that with your Sunday jeans."

"Don't forget the card." Lexi handed Hunter the envelope attached to the torn wrapping paper.

Hunter read the card to himself and his eyes began to fill with tears.

"What's wrong, honey?" Lexi wrapped her arm protectively around his shoulder. "Why are you upset?"

"I've never been away from my family on my birthday before and I miss them," Hunter confessed. "Plus they call this my Gotcha Day."

"Your Gotcha Day?" Shane asked.

"It's the day they adopted me. My brother and sister are adopted, too."

Hunter's indifference surprised Lexi. She was also surprised Clay hadn't uncovered the other adoptions. He might have if she'd given him the go-ahead to keep digging.

No one asked any questions and Hunter didn't expand any further. He was a normal, well-adjusted kid with a loving family and that was the best gift she could give to her child.

"Now's your chance to get her car," Hunter whispered to Shane when Lexi started to clean up the picnic table. "I can keep her busy."

"I don't want to leave in the middle of your party."

"I'm a man now, I can take care of myself," Hunter drawled. "And this is a get-together. I'm too old for parties. She still has her bathing suit on so I'll ask her to go swimming again in the river."

Sneaking across the corral, ducking behind horses, Shane hoped no one noticed the extra set of legs running by. He knew Lexi always left the keys under the seat in case she had an emergency and had to leave quickly.

He didn't have time to wash and wax it himself, but he did have time to drive down the highway to Bubba's Bubbles and get it detailed.

The line for the car wash started all the way down the street. If Shane had any chance of getting Lexi's car back soon, this wasn't going to cut it. He dialed the number on the sign, and a woman answered.

"Darla? It's Shane Langtry. Do you think that husband of yours can do me a favor?"

Two hours later, he was back on the road. Hunter had texted him thirty minutes ago that Lexi was receiving some business phone calls but so far none of them were emergencies. This was a good thing considering he had her medical bags in the car with him. Hopefully he'd return before she missed them. He had to give Hunter credit, the kid was a good partner in crime.

He glanced at the glove box and wondered what else she might have in the car. Reaching over he tried the latch but it was locked. Looking at the steering column, he saw the key on her key ring. If he pulled off the road and opened the lock, he'd learn what she had not so successfully been hiding. *And he'd be a first-class jackass.*

Shane caught a woman going through his phone once and that was enough for him to kick her to the curb. Curiosity was one thing, but respect was another and he wasn't going to violate Lexi's trust that way. Then again, he was driving around in a car he'd technically stolen so that didn't say much about him.

Stopping at the ranch entrance, he texted Hunter to make sure Lexi couldn't see the main drive or parking area. Pulling into the same spot she'd parked in, he tossed her keys under the seat and snuck back toward the barbecue pits.

"Where on earth have you been?" Kay grabbed hold of him behind the bunkhouse. "How dare you sneak out of here when this was your idea."

"I took Lexi's car to get detailed." Shane loved the shocked expression on his mother's face. "Hunter was in on it, too. Do me a favor and tell Lexi one of the grooms noticed she has a flat tire."

Shane crept through the bushes on the other side of the pits so he'd be able to saunter in inconspicuously.

"Really?" Lexi listened to Kay and sighed. "Those are fairly new tires."

"What's wrong?" Shane slipped in beside her, signaling to Hunter, who was standing nearby with some of the other students.

"Where'd you come from?" Lexi looked around. "Never mind, someone told your mom I have a flat tire and I was going down to check it out."

"Hunter and I can change it for you," Shane offered. "Isn't that right?"

"You can change it, I'll supervise." Hunter grinned. "It's my birthday."

"Thanks, kid." Shane appreciated the added cover.

They hiked down to the parking area and Lexi walked all around her car, looking at each tire. "I don't see a flat, do you?"

"Are you sure that's your car?" Shane asked, trying not to laugh.

"Yeah, it looks too clean to be yours," Hunter added.

"Of course this is—how did my car get so clean?" Lexi ran her hand over the trunk. "Waxed, too?"

"Must have been the car fairy." Hunter peered in the windows. "Even the inside's clean."

"Did you do this?" Lexi poked Shane in the chest. "Is that where you've been?"

Shane sheepishly nodded, not sure if she was pleased or mad. "I'm repaying you for when you did mine."

"Well, it sure took you long enough." Lexi reached up and kissed him on the cheek while Hunter gave him the thumbs-up from the other side of the car. "Thank you."

"I'd do anything to see you smile," Shane said. "Someday I'll prove just how much you mean to me, and when I do, you'll finally understand we were meant to be together."

FAMILY DAY WAS in full swing at the Ride 'em High! Rodeo School when Lexi drove into the ranch. She'd made the decision last night to stay away because she didn't want the pain of seeing her son with his adopted family. Curiosity got the best of her somewhere between "don't do it" and "just a peek won't hurt."

A peek it was. Grabbing her medical bag from the back of the car, she had the excuse to be there without looking suspicious. Not that she'd ever look suspicious at Bridle Dance, but she was overly paranoid and hoped no one caught on to her fear.

Walking through the stables, she turned the corner and faced Shane, Hunter and his family looking in at Apollo. Immediately regretting her decision, Lexi spun on her heels and tried to retreat before anyone saw her.

"Lexi, wait!" Hunter called out to her. "I want you to meet my parents."

Lexi took a deep breath and slowly turned to meet the Rathbones…the people raising her son. She had opted for a closed adoption but she couldn't be certain what the Rathbones knew about her. Slowly she reached out for what seemed like an eternity and shook the hand of the woman her son called Mom.

"It's nice to meet you," Lexi said.

The woman's head tilted slightly and the handshake lingered longer than it should have, making Lexi increasingly nervous.

"*Our* son tells us you're a veterinarian," Mrs. Rathbone said.

Paranoia be damned, there was a definite emphasis on the word *our*. Lexi didn't know how but she was almost certain the woman knew who she was. Maybe it was intuition, maybe the adoption agency revealed more about her than they should have, but the fear and anger in the woman's eyes told Lexi she needed to get the hell out of there.

"I'm sorry, I have an emergency." Lexi made a beeline for the side door and sprinted past two corrals to her car. Fumbling with the key, she started the engine and peeled out of there before anyone caught up with her.

She dialed Clay's number and he answered on the second ring.

"They know." Lexi began to hyperventilate and forced herself to pull down a side road and stop the car.

"Who knows?" Clay asked.

Lexi tried to calm her ragged breaths.

"Breathe, Lexi," Clay soothed. "Are you home?"

"No." *Breathe in, breathe out.*

"Are you at the ranch?"

"No, I left," she croaked. "The Rathbones are here."

"For Family Day, right?" he asked. "I'm not even going to ask why you went there. I probably would have done the same thing. Did you tell them or did they figure it out?"

"When she heard my name," Lexi sobbed. "She knew. What have I done?"

"Don't jump to any conclusions, Lex. How far are you from home?"

"Ten minutes."

"I'll meet you there," Clay said. "Can you manage to drive there?"

"Y-yes. I'll be in the stables."

"Sit tight, Lex. I'm on my way."

LEXI LED AUTUMN into the barn and started to brush her. She thanked the stars that she usually had the stables to herself with the exception of Nash when he wanted to ride. She didn't have to worry about anyone invading her space and she could breathe a little easier.

She heard Clay's truck roll in and she was glad she had him to confide in.

"I see you got here in one piece." Clay smiled but Lexi didn't have it in her to return the smile.

"They're probably telling Shane right now."

"Even if they know who you are they have no way of knowing he's Hunter's father."

"They know." Lexi stopped brushing Autumn and closed her eyes. "Because they just pulled in the driveway."

"THAT WAS A blast today." Shane sauntered into the kitchen and popped a pod in the coffee machine. "I think I'm really cut out for this whole teaching gig."

"You certainly surprised me." Kay held Barney out in front of her and started talking to him. "I didn't think he'd have the patience. Did you? No, you didn't."

"Yup, she's lost it." Shane laughed.

"I know I fought you and Chase on this, but I'm proud of you two." Cole joined Chase at the counter. "You've impressed me."

"Thanks, I think." Shane took a sip of coffee. "Has anyone heard from Lexi? She said she had an emergency and tore out of here."

"I hope it was nothing too bad," Tess said. "Although it wouldn't be an emergency if it wasn't serious."

"I might call her in a few if I don't hear anything," Shane said. "I can't tell you how many people told me today that Hunter and I look alike. The kid definitely has potential on the circuit. After I speak to his parents, I'm going to see if Brock wants to rep him. They seem like nice people but they're completely clueless when it comes to the rodeo."

"Have you stopped to think about why Hunter might look and act so much like you?" his mother asked.

"The kid idolizes me," Shane bragged. "I'm sure he picked up my mannerisms along the way."

"I think he did, too, but I don't believe it came from watching you," Kay said.

"I've been thinking the same thing," Cole added. "I think he comes by them naturally."

Shane laughed. "What are you implying? That Hunter's my kid? I was married to Sharon and I assure you, I didn't touch anyone while we were married, including Sharon."

"You weren't married to her nine months before Hunter was born. You married Sharon in November," Cole said.

"Hunter would have been conceived in October," Kay added.

"Okay, so I was with Lexi." Shane thought back to

the month before he married Sharon. To the weekend he spent with Lexi at Devil's Thumb…when Lexi attended Colorado State.

"What are you saying?" Tess laughed. "We—or someone—certainly would have noticed if Lexi was pregnant when she came home from school for the holidays, at least by spring break and definitely by the summer."

"She didn't come home," Shane mumbled.

"What did you say, Shane?" Cole asked. "I didn't hear you."

"She didn't come home until August, right before she transferred to Cornell."

"CAN I HELP YOU?" Clay called out from the barn door.

"Is Lexi here?" the man asked. "That is her car, isn't it?"

"We need to talk to her," the woman said.

Clay looked toward Lexi in the shadows. "Your call."

Lexi exhaled sharply. "Let's get this over with."

Clay stepped aside so Mr. and Mrs. Rathbone were able to see her. They walked across the yard toward her and then just stopped and stared.

"I'm Clay." At least someone broke the ice.

"I'm Dennis and this is my wife, Melissa. We're Hunter's parents."

Lexi stiffened at the word but forced herself to meet their gaze. "How did you figure it out?"

"We didn't know much concerning Hunter's biological mother but we did know her name was Alexis," Melissa said. "That she was from Texas and studying to be a veterinarian. All this time Hunter was telling us about a vet named Lexi and it didn't dawn on me that you were

Alexis until I saw him next to you. I immediately saw you in him and I knew."

"I promise I won't interfere in his life," Lexi said. "I had no idea he was coming here. This was as much a shock to me as it was to you."

"So this wasn't your and Shane's plan?" Melissa spat. "Because I'm assuming he's the father now that I've seen the three of you together. How was this going to work? You get him down here for a month and try to take him from us?"

"Definitely not. I wasn't even sure he was my son. I had to hire Clay to find out."

"Hire him?" Dennis asked. "What are you?"

"I'm a private investigator, sir, and I can assure you, Lexi did not plan this. She's been agonizing over this for weeks and she had decided not to say a word to anyone about it."

"Oh, sure." Melissa rolled her eyes and folded her arms across her chest. "You don't think we honestly believe that?"

"The reason I gave you my son, and yes, I *gave you my son,* was because I wanted a better life for him. I want him to be happy and I'm not going to do anything to jeopardize that."

"At least now it makes sense why Shane's taken such an interest in Hunter," Dennis said, fuming at Lexi. "Does he even think he has any talent or was this just to get close to him?"

"I didn't even know Hunter was mine and Shane didn't, either. He still doesn't know he has a son."

Her confession brought immediate silence.

"Yes, I'm the horrible woman who gave her son up for adoption and didn't even tell the father she was pregnant. I had my reasons and I stand by them today. He's your son. I won't do anything to change that."

"It's not that simple," Melissa said. "All of our kids are adopted and we have a no-secret policy in our family. We told them if their parents ever surfaced, we wouldn't keep it from them. I'm not going to break that promise to Hunter. He has a right to choose if he wants a relationship with you and Shane. We're not going to make that choice for him."

"I admire your decision, but please give me some time to tell Shane."

"We'll give you a few hours," Melissa said.

"What?" Lexi sputtered.

"What's the rush?" Clay asked. "Why can't you give her a few days?"

"We get on a plane to go home tomorrow," Dennis said. "We need to give Hunter some time to decide if he wants to get on that plane with us."

"Do you have a number where I can reach you?" Lexi's hands shook as she removed her business card out of her wallet and handed it to them. "My mobile number is on the bottom."

"I think I should drive you to the ranch," Clay said after the Rathbones left.

Lexi shook her head and calmly sat down on the hay bale near Autumn's stall. Covering her eyes, she cried.

"I lied to both of them," she sobbed. "And now I have to break Shane's heart. I never wanted to hurt anyone. I just wanted my son to be happy."

"I WAS JUST about to call and check up on you," Shane said when he saw Lexi walk up to the corral where the boys practiced roping. "They're really good. Hunter and Tyler show the most potential. What do you think?"

Shane glanced sideways at Lexi when she didn't respond. Sunglasses covering her eyes, she stood and watched.

"Everything all right with your emergency?" Shane had a strong suspicion what that emergency was, considering the Rathbones left shortly after she did.

Lexi nodded. "Um, I don't know yet."

"You know how everyone keeps saying how much Hunter looks like me?" Shane turned his back toward the corral fence, placed a booted foot on the bottom rail and hoisted himself to sit on the top. "You're going to love this—my mom and Cole have this wild idea that you had a secret kid when you were away at Colorado State. Isn't that a hoot?" He quickly glanced down at Lexi, but she only stared out into the corral. "I did the math, and that meant you would have been pregnant when I married Sharon and I told them there was no way in hell you'd have allowed that to happen if you were carrying my child. That's insane, right, Lexi? You'd never do something that horrible to me, would you?"

"It's not insane, Shane."

Seething, he said, "Just say it!"

"Hunter is your son." Lexi shook her head. "He's our son."

Shane hopped off the fence and turned her to face him.

"I have a son and you kept it from me for thirteen years?" Confirming what he already knew made the situation that much more painful. "I was wrong. There is someone worse than Sharon—you."

Chapter Eleven

Shane gripped Lexi by the arm and led her away from the round pen and toward the parking area. The last person he wanted to overhear the conversation about his real parents was Hunter since it was obvious the kid had no idea he was his father.

"How could you do this to me?" Shane growled, still holding on to her arm. "What right did you have to take my child away from me?"

"I was eighteen." Lexi pulled away from him. "I came home to tell you but before I opened my mouth you told me you cheated on me, got Sharon pregnant and oh, by the way, we're getting married in a few days. Happy Thanksgiving to me!"

"That doesn't excuse what you did." He couldn't believe she was trying to talk her way out of this.

"You made it very clear to me that day that you and I were no longer together. That you had a responsibility to your child and you were going to see it through. Think back to that afternoon, Shane. What did I say to you? Nothing! You wouldn't even let me speak. Once again, it was the *Shane Show* and it was all about you and the damn rodeo. News flash—I made it about our son and did what was right for him."

"By keeping him from me?" Shane removed his hat and waved it in the air. "How was that the right thing to do?"

"I couldn't raise him on my own. I was in school and I was staying in school."

"You were selfish," Shane spat. "You thought only about yourself. Don't you dare say you did this for Hunter."

"I was selfish?" Lexi laughed. "Who couldn't keep it in his pants? Hmm, I think that was pretty selfish on your part. And who couldn't use birth control? Ding, ding, ding, right again. So don't give me the 'I'm selfish' crap."

Shane didn't believe the words coming out of her mouth. He made a mistake, but it didn't justify giving their son up for adoption. Not when he was willing to be a parent.

"I would have raised him if you were so dead set on going to school."

"Now that's funny. Sometimes I have to laugh at all these recollections you seem to have of Dylan because you were never around. You were constantly on the road plus you had your hands full with a buckle-bunny tramp of a wife. You barely handled that. There was no way you'd be able to deal with another child."

"I was there for Dylan." How dare she say he wasn't. He'd loved that child more than he loved anyone. It was a different love than what he'd felt for Lexi, which was nonexistent now.

"I was even thinking about this at the Fourth of July picnic," Lexi went on, "and how once again you weren't around. You've never been around longer than a few weeks in a row and even that's a stretch. So don't you dare accuse me of being selfish and for wanting to stay in school. You were born rich and you'll die rich, but in the end you're a rodeo cowboy in his thirties who doesn't give a crap about anyone else except himself."

"Now I've lost two kids."

"Blame yourself for that." Lexi walked toward her car. "Tell me, what would you have changed about your life, if you had known about Hunter?"

Shane slapped his hat against his thigh as he tried to come up with an answer. He knew many rodeo cowboys with families at home and he also knew many that retired early to be with their families.

"I would have made it work." Shane sat on the tree stump in front of Lexi's car. The cut was fresh, but he didn't remember when the tree was taken down. *It must have happened when I was...away.* "I'm not gone *all* the time, but yes, I'm on the road a lot. How else am I going to win the championship?"

"I, I, I!" Lexi stomped her foot for emphasis. "Listen to yourself. It's all about you and the rodeo—what you want, what you need, what makes Shane happy. You say you've changed, but you haven't. No one wants this stupid rodeo reality show and yet you're shoving it down everyone's throats. Why? Because Shane Langtry has to be in the spotlight all the time."

"That's not true." Shane jumped to his feet.

"Really?" Lexi stepped toward him, inches from his face. "Where's Chase in all the talk about the TV show? You never mention him."

Shane felt his blood pressure skyrocket. He'd been furious with Sharon, but it was nothing compared to the anger he felt toward Lexi. The one woman he loved, the one person he trusted, and she'd betrayed him. *You betrayed her first.*

He needed to get away from her before he did something they'd both regret.

"Get out of here," Shane snarled. "I don't want to see you here again. You're fired."

"Oh, please. Is that your reality-show training kicking in? You can't fire me because I don't work for you. I own my own practice and if your family chooses not to use me again, then so be it. But just so you know, the Rathbones are on their way to tell Hunter."

"They're coming now?" Shane looked toward their son, who was laughing and swinging his rope high in the air.

"Yes."

"Unbelievable." Shane thought she'd done the worst to him. This just confirmed it. "You're only telling me because you got caught."

Lexi nodded. "You're right. If they hadn't found out, I wouldn't have told you. I was not going to disrupt his life, and he has a great life, with a wonderful family, which is more than we would have been able to give him."

"I never had the chance."

"Neither did I," Lexi thundered. "You took my chance away the night you cheated on me, only I didn't know it then. Instead, you let me live a lie and then shattered my world when you told me you created a family with someone else. What I did was never about another man. It was about an innocent child that didn't deserve to be brought up in the middle of a battlefield."

"You can't even say you're sorry, can you?"

Lexi shook her head. "I stand by what I did and I make no apologies for it."

A tan SUV parked in front of the rodeo school. The Rathbones remained in the car, watching their son practice. *Their son.* Shane's parental rights had been stripped from him without his knowledge and he had to accept it. Even he knew no judge worth his salt would give Shane back his son, and even if that happened, Hunter would resent Shane. There was literally nothing he could do about any of it.

"I'm sure you want to talk to the Rathbones." Lexi slid behind the wheel of her convertible. "They're good people, Shane. I had them background-checked and their first priority is—"

Shane raised his hand to stop her from speaking. "You had them background-checked? When? Then or recently?"

He watched Lexi swallow hard, knowing she'd said more than she had intended to. "That SOB." Shane tightened his hands into a first. "My best friend knew Hunter was my son and didn't tell me?"

Lexi slowly nodded. "I had to be certain."

"And like you said, if you hadn't been caught, you wouldn't have told me, right?"

"Right." Lexi didn't blink. She just stared at him, devoid of all emotion. He had to hand it to her, she'd mastered the doctor's "I have bad news" expression perfectly.

"You asked Clay to lie to me?"

"I asked Clay to do a job for me, and yes, I wondered how you'd react if you found out. Clay said you'd understand it was his job. That's how much faith he put in the strength of your relationship."

"Stop trying to sugarcoat it." Shane stepped away from her car. "You both betrayed me. I'm such a fool— here I thought maybe you were sleeping together, not keeping my child from me."

LEXI WAS RIGHT. Shane hated her for giving up their son and she'd broken his heart. She didn't mean for it to happen that way, but it was the right decision at the time.

Upon seeing the Rathbones drive onto the ranch, Lexi decided it was best to leave them alone to talk, without her. She called Ashleigh and told her to check on Bridle Dance's horses and to call her if there were any problems. Come tomorrow the Langtrys would probably have another equine vet and she'd have to live with it.

She needed to get past today, and if telling Shane was hard, telling her family might be worse. Parking behind the Bed & Biscuit, she started to climb the Victorian's back stairs.

"Lexi?" A woman's voice called her name. "Over here, at the vet's office."

Lexi squinted across Mazie's backyard and saw Kay standing next to her Mercedes with Barney in her arms. Bracing herself for another onslaught, Lexi negotiated her sister's agility obstacle course for dogs, unlatched the gate and stepped into Dr. Cerf's parking lot.

"Hello, Kay." Lexi reached out and scratched Barney under the chin. "Hello, Barney."

"We had a great vet visit today." Kay kissed the poodle pup on the top of the head. "He got another shot and he's up to twelve pounds."

"That's great." Lexi was surprised at Kay's nonchalance, considering Shane told her his mother and Cole had figured out the truth. "How did you know?"

"He told you, huh?" Kay shifted Barney in her arms. "Can I put him down?"

"I wouldn't." Lexi shook her head. "Sick animals come to a vet's and you don't want a puppy that's not fully immunized to touch the grounds or the floor inside."

"So it's true, then?" Kay's tone was surprisingly unaccusatory while she transferred the puppy from one arm to the other.

"It is and I'm sure you have plenty of questions." Lexi steeled herself once more, ready to hear how ungrateful she was when Joe gave her the gift of a lifetime by bringing her home and setting up her lab. Or how her husband died without knowing his grandson. But Kay didn't say anything.

The woman reached up and gave Lexi a hug, Barney between them, licking at her.

"Being a mother is the toughest job in the world." Kay drew back and held Lexi's chin. "I know you did what you thought was best for Hunter. Shane made a mess of things and his father and I only added to it when we told him he needed to do right by Sharon and marry her. We never should have forced that issue."

"I can't believe I'm hearing this." Tears welled in Lexi's eyes.

"Don't get me wrong, Lexi," Kay warned. "I'm not excusing you for not coming to Shane and discussing this, but I do understand why you didn't. You made a good choice for Hunter. I can't tell you it was the best choice because no one knows that, but you put his needs before your own and he seems very well-adjusted."

"Giving him up was the hardest thing I ever had to do, and please understand I didn't just keep this from your family. My family doesn't know either and I need to tell them today. The sooner the better, considering the Rathbones are with Shane now and they plan on telling Hunter everything."

"I should be getting home then." Kay opened her car door, fanning the inside. "Oh, it's hot in there. Call me if you need my help and remember, Lexi, we love you."

"Even after all this?" Lexi asked.

Kay smiled. "Remind me one day to tell you some of the crap Joe pulled for love. Give Shane some time, he'll come around…I promise."

That definitely wasn't the conversation she expected to have with Kay. Two down, many more to go, but Lexi didn't think her heart could handle another one-on-one confession. She needed to round up her entire family, tell them all together and pull the Band-Aid off in one fell swoop.

Letting herself in Mazie's back door, she found her sister in the kitchen, baking as usual. Forever taking care of everyone else. Lexi wondered what her sister would have done if it had been her instead of Lexi. Knowing Mazie, she would have strapped the kid on her back and gone about her daily routine. Domestication suited her perfectly, just like it did Vicki Slater and now Miranda. And maybe if it had happened to Lexi at this age, things might have turned out differently, but at eighteen she wasn't ready for anything more serious than a textbook.

"Are you all right?" her sister asked while rolling out a pie crust, not bothering to look up. "Your conversation with Kay seemed pretty intense out there."

"Can you come to the farm tonight around nine? I need to call a family meeting."

Mazie stopped rolling and met her gaze. "Lexi,

what's wrong?" Mazie wiped her hands on a nearby dish towel. "You look terrible."

"Trust me when I say I feel even worse."

"Are you sick?" Mazie ushered Lexi toward a chair and forced her to sit down, quickly testing her cheek with the back of her hand to see if she had a temperature. "Whatever it is, we'll find you the best doctors."

"Mazie." Lexi grabbed her sister's hands. "My overly dramatic little sister, I'm not sick. I do need to tell everyone something tonight and I need your help. Do you think you can do that without asking too many questions?"

"I—I guess." Mazie sat down at the table. "Why are you being so cryptic?"

Lexi laughed. "And the questions already begin. Maybe I should have gone to Nash."

"No, don't—I'm sorry," Mazie said. "What am I saying, I'm not sorry. You're my sister, something's obviously wrong and I've been worried about you lately. Ever since that rodeo school opened, you've been distant and kind of bitchy." Mazie's hand flew to her mouth. "It's that kid, isn't it? The one that looks so much like Shane. Don't tell me—he had another affair while you two were together, didn't he? There's been talk around town that Hunter was his long lost son. Who is she? Is it someone we know?"

"Yes...very well."

"I'M SURE YOU understand we have questions," Dennis Rathbone said to Shane outside the rodeo school entrance. "After we tell Hunter, Melissa and I are going to want to sit down with both you and Lexi to sort this mess out. I can't begin to tell you how distrustful we are of this situation."

"So you already have a judgment about who I am?" Shane thought he'd at least have a chance to tell them his side of the story before they took Hunter back to the hotel. He guessed he should be thankful they hadn't packed Hunter's belongings yet. Shane wanted to consider the fact that they left their two younger kids at the ranch with Hunter while they tracked down Lexi as a sign they had some trust in him. "This doesn't paint me in a good light considering I was the one Lexi kept this from all these years. I'm not some horrible monster of a parent."

"We don't know what to think or believe and I don't feel comfortable leaving Hunter here with you until we know more," Melissa said, her anger obvious. "You have to admit, this doesn't look good for either one of you. And that private investigator she hired. What's to say she didn't hire him to find Hunter? You could both be in on this."

"Then get all the facts," Shane pleaded. "I was married to someone else when Hunter was born. Lexi went away to school and stayed away until after she gave him up for adoption. I didn't know she was pregnant. No one did."

Melissa and Dennis regarded him for a while before Melissa finally spoke. "Lexi disappears for nine months and no one suspects anything?"

"It's not as simple as you're making it out to be." Shane wanted a chance to know his son, to spend more time with him. He'd go to hell and back not to get shut out again.

"We're going to tell Hunter the truth first," Dennis

said. "And then we'll let him decide if he wants a relationship with you and Lexi. This is his choice alone, but we will supervise any communication and we have the final say if something seems even remotely off."

"Fair enough," Shane agreed. "Thank you. Not just for this, but for raising an incredible kid. Excuse me."

Shane didn't want to see Hunter walk away knowing he might never see him again. He'd already lived that pain once. He heard footsteps behind and turned, hoping to see Hunter chasing after him.

"What's going on?" Chase asked. "Why were you and Lexi arguing and why are you so upset?"

"Because that kid…" Shane saw Hunter meet the Rathbones at the fence rail. "The kid that looks so much like me…*is my son.* And there isn't a damn thing I can do about it."

"You have to be joking." Chase looked from Hunter to Shane. "Aren't those his parents?"

"Guess you weren't there when he told us he was adopted during his birthday get-together. None of this makes any sense. The night Apollo was born she was scared to death to touch Hunter."

"You're losing me." Chase placed his hands on Shane's shoulders. "Is Ashleigh his mother? Wow, she had to be his age when she had him. How could you?"

"What?" Shane pulled away from Chase. "Not Ashleigh—Lexi. Lexi is Hunter's mother."

"But how? She was never pregnant."

"Well, apparently she was, because she gave birth to him when she was still at Colorado State and the Rathbones adopted him. She kept one hell of a secret from me. Never in a million years would I have guessed this one."

"I can't believe it." Chase removed his hat and scratched his head. "Hunter's really yours and Lexi's."

"It's so crazy even I don't believe it," Shane said. "But there's more. Someone else knew about it and didn't tell me."

"Who?"

"Clay." Shane wanted to wring the man's neck. "Some friend, huh? Turns out he's been helping her."

"Helping her do what?" Chase asked.

"To cover it up, I guess." Shane paced back and forth on the walkway. "I haven't spoken to Clay yet."

"That doesn't sound like him at all." Chase put his arm around Shane's shoulder and led him toward the parking area. "Clay uncovers things, not hides them."

"Lexi said he helped her confirm Hunter's paternity."

"Now that makes more sense," Chase agreed. "I think you need to stop jumping to conclusions and speak with Clay."

A car started and Shane and Chase watched the Rathbones rental SUV drive out of the parking lot. A piece of his heart felt like it had just been torn from his body.

"Where are they going?"

"Back to their hotel, where they can tell Hunter that we are his biological parents and then he will decide if he wants further contact with us. How could she do this to me?"

Shane knew his brother was right. He had to talk to Clay and hear his side of the story the same way he'd asked the Rathbones to listen to his. But his best friend? He could have overlooked almost anything but keeping his kid from him…that was unforgivable.

Twenty minutes later, Shane found himself knocking on Clay's front door.

"Hey, man," Clay greeted him. "Since when do you knock or come in the front door?"

"How long have you known Hunter is my son?"

"I wondered when you were going to show up." Clay held the door open for Shane. "I got the DNA results before Hunter's birthday."

"You DNA tested my son?" Shane snorted. "Why didn't you tell me?"

"Because it wasn't my place. Lexi hired me to do a job, Shane. It was never about you."

"How can you say that?" Shane yelled. "Now you sound like Lexi."

"Because it's the truth. Lexi came to me the day she first saw Hunter. She wasn't going to say anything to anyone until she knew for sure, and honestly, Shane, Lexi thought she was doing what was best for Hunter."

Clay walked into the kitchen and took two beers out of the fridge.

"Enough with the stall tactics, please. Lexi isn't going to miraculously appear and save you." Unless Clay was waiting for her to show up. "Let me guess, she's on her way."

"She might be." Clay shrugged, twisted the top off his beer and handed one to Shane. "I don't know where she is or where she's going. I haven't spoken to or seen her since the Rathbones confronted her at her house. I'm still trying to figure out who told them where she lived."

"What did her family have to say about this? Or, did they know from the get-go? Is that why they hate me so much? Did they keep her away while she was pregnant and then force her to give the baby up because it was mine?"

"Listen to you," Clay laughed. "Quite a conspiracy

theory you have going on there. Her parents hate you because you were a dog and hurt their daughter when you married your pregnant one-night stand. They didn't know then and they don't know now. Well, they might now if she came clean to them after she told you."

"Then tell me what I'm missing." Shane placed the unopened beer on the coffee table and sat down on the couch. "Be my friend and tell me."

"There's nothing left to tell you." Clay stood firm. "There was no plot against you. She didn't know what to do with the information. She was scared and alone and I was the one she turned to. I was also the furthest removed from the situation. If that bothers you, I'm sorry, but at least it was me and not someone else. I would never betray either one of you."

"I have to ask you this and I hate like hell that I do." Shane had heard the rumors around town that Lexi spent the night with Clay and now he needed to hear the truth for himself. "Please be straight with me. Did you sleep with Lexi?"

"How can you even ask me that?" Clay's wounded expression made Shane feel like a first-class jerk.

Soon, Shane found himself driving east on the interstate, wanting to put as many miles between him and Ramblewood as possible. An hour later, he pulled into a truck stop to refuel and think. He ordered a burger and Coke but hardly touched either one. Watching the cars and trucks barrel down the highway, Shane remembered the first time he got the bug.

He and his family were sitting in a roadside restaurant, not unlike this one, somewhere in Louisiana. They were on the way back from one of their vacations and Shane stared out the window wondering where everyone was going. He wanted to travel and see the country and the rodeo would definitely take him there.

It had its up and downs, but in the end he'd accomplished everything he set out to do, except win the world all-around title. This year he had a solid chance and he wasn't going to let anyone stand in his way.

What about Hunter?

What was he going to do if Hunter said he wanted a relationship with him? Denver was only a two-hour flight away, so it would be feasible to be present for all Hunter's events. Besides that, Shane had contemplated representing Hunter, being his agent. But that also would entail scaling back his own rodeo time and he wanted that championship so bad he could taste it. The world all-around title had been his dream since he first sat on a horse. He'd be the first Langtry to win the title and Chase was right there beside him in the standings. Shane had to get there first, then Chase could win it ten times over, but he had to be first.

And this was what Lexi meant.

"Dammit!" Shane slammed his fist on the table.

"I'm sorry, is there something wrong with your food, sir?" the waitress asked.

Embarrassed, Shane glanced around the restaurant and realized he had an audience. He lowered his head and tried to sink down in the booth. "No, ma'am. My apologies, I'm just having a rough day. May I have my check?"

Leaving the woman a generous tip, Shane drove back to Ramblewood and asked Lexi to meet with him. Reluctantly she agreed on the condition they talk and not yell at each other.

Shane wanted to hear about her pregnancy, Hunter's

birth, everything on the background check. He needed to know all he could about *his son*. The question was, would she talk to him after the way he treated her?

LEXI WAITED IN the car for Shane, choosing the ball field as a neutral location. She had two hours before she faced her family.

Shane parked next to her and they both got out of their cars.

"Thanks for meeting me," Shane said. "Have you heard anything?"

"No." Lexi wondered if he had, and if he'd even tell her. "You?"

Shane shook his head and started to walk. She joined him, and the sounds of baseball bats striking balls and kids' laughter made Lexi second-guess her choice of locations.

"Was it a difficult pregnancy?" Shane asked.

Surprised at the question, she thought back to the days she tried so hard to forget. "Uncomfortable when it got warmer, but other than that I still went to class every day and continued working. Twenty-two hours of labor, that was a different story altogether."

Shane couldn't even imagine what that was like. "What did you do with all the ultrasound pictures from your appointments?"

"I didn't have any."

"What?" Shane stopped her. "You didn't go to the doctor?"

Lexi shook her head and continued to walk. "I mean I didn't have any photos." Lexi didn't want to see her baby before or after it was born. "The doctors knew I was giving him up for adoption so I chose not to see him. I heard the heartbeat and I knew it was a boy when he was born, but that was it. I never laid eyes on Hunter until a few weeks ago."

"How did you know it was him?"

"The resemblance to you was uncanny, and then when your mom told me he was from Colorado I started to ask more questions, then I begged Clay to find out for sure."

When Shane didn't comment, Lexi braved a glance at him. His jaw tight, she knew he wanted to say more and didn't.

"I put Clay in that position, so if you're going to be mad at someone, make it me, not him."

"I'm not mad." Shane stopped walking and looked toward the softball game. "I'm disappointed that you thought so little of me that you had to hide our son."

"And I'm disappointed in how you handled it, but what good does that do us today?" Lexi turned to walk back toward her car. "I'm not going to play the 'blame game' again."

"How am I supposed to react?" Shane asked. "Please tell me so I can get something right this time."

"I don't know what to tell you."

Lexi's phone vibrated in her pocket. She mouthed "it's them" as she answered the phone.

"Hello."

"Lexi, it's Melissa."

"How are you?" Lexi asked, knowing they were probably anxious as well.

"We're still trying to understand the chain of events." Melissa's tone was curt. "We weren't expecting to ever meet Hunter's parents. Honestly, he's never expressed an interest in knowing who you are."

"Oh." The words stung. Shane stood in front of her, trying to read her expressions.

"I'm sorry." Melissa sighed. "I don't mean to hurt you, but we have a fairly normal life and this took us by surprise."

"Us, too." Lexi wasn't sure where the conversation was leading. Afraid to ask any questions for fear she'd chase off Melissa, Lexi allowed the other woman to steer the conversation.

"We've spoken with Hunter and told him you and Shane are his biological parents, and if you agree, he would like to have some form of a relationship with you."

"Yes!" Lexi kneeled to the ground, looking up with tears spilling onto her cheeks. "Yes, it's more than okay. We'd love to have a relationship with him."

Chapter Twelve

"So you're my dad?" Hunter said, sizing up Shane across the table. "Now you know where you get your good looks from."

Shane laughed. "That I do."

The Rathbones reluctantly agreed to allow Hunter to finish out the rodeo program, but only if they were all able to sit down in the morning and discuss the situation. Until their meeting, they wanted Hunter to stay with them at the hotel. Lexi and Shane agreed, but Shane asked if he could meet with Hunter for a few minutes tonight.

Sitting a couple of tables away in the hotel restaurant, Dennis and Melissa protectively watched Shane's interaction with their son. Lexi wanted to join them but explained to Hunter that she had to make things right with her own family and promised to see him tomorrow. Hunter must have inherited his maturity from Lexi because the boy had twice the amount at thirteen that Shane had at that age.

"I can't wait to go back to school and tell all my friends who you are," Hunter said.

"Your mom and dad are okay with you telling people about me?" With his reputation, he was surprised the Rathbones didn't grab Hunter and run in the opposite direction. He hadn't exactly been an angel, but to people outside of the rodeo circuit, he was just another Texas cowboy.

"Oh, yeah." Hunter looked over to them and waved. "I know they look uptight, but they're really not. I mean we can't get away with cutting school or eating pizza for dinner every night, but I know I can talk to them about anything. My sister, Amelia, has known her mom since she was born. She even comes to holiday dinners."

"Really?" Shane was amazed at how casually they took adoption. "If she's still that involved, why didn't she just raise your sister?"

"Adults make things too complicated." Hunter twisted his straw wrapper. "Amelia's mom was seventeen when my sister was born. She wanted to graduate and go on to college—kind of like Lexi. Her parents got a lawyer who told my parents they could adopt Amelia but her mom wanted her to know who she was. I think they call it an open adoption. So my sister has our mom and she has her bonus mom. Now I'll have a bonus mom, too."

"You're amazing." Shane almost found it impossible to take his eyes off his son. "How'd you get so smart?"

"It's in my genes. My mom's a doctor, ya know." Hunter smiled. "She's telling her family about me tonight, huh? Do you think they'll like me?"

"Are you kidding me? They'll love you," Shane reassured him. "Lexi's family lives on a farm and they have a big country store and a petting zoo."

"Are they going to be mad?" Hunter furrowed his brow. "Lexi's parents?"

"Mmm, I'm not sure how they're going to react."

Shane checked his watch. It was quarter to nine and he knew she must be nervous.

"Maybe you should be there," Hunter said. "You're kinda responsible for the situation."

"Yeah." Shane wrinkled his nose. "I kinda was."

LEXI'S ENTIRE FAMILY sat in the living room, curious as to what the emergency meeting that Mazie called to order was about.

"There's something I need to tell all of you so I'm just going to say it." Lexi inhaled and let out a long slow breath. "I had a baby when I was eighteen and gave it up for adoption."

There. Band-Aid off.

"You did what?" Judy Lawson approached her daughter. "You had a baby?"

Lexi backed away from her mother. Okay, so maybe this wasn't the best approach.

"Mom." Nash stepped between the two of them. "Sit down and let Lexi explain." He turned to look at her. "You are going to explain, right?"

"There's not a whole to say and getting mad at me isn't going to solve anything, either."

"Is this one of those 'I didn't know I was pregnant' stories?" her aunt Heidi asked. "I never did understand how that was possible."

"I knew I was pregnant all along and I had planned on telling Shane."

"Shane?" everyone said in unison.

"Well, yes, who else would it have been?"

"That makes it even worse," her father said.

"Why didn't you tell me?" Mazie scolded. "I would have been there for you."

"Because you were sixteen."

"I knew she shouldn't have gone away to school," her Uncle Ed said. "There were perfectly fine schools here."

"Did he make you keep this a secret?" her mother asked.

"No, of course not." These were the hundred questions she didn't want to face. "He didn't know because I didn't tell him."

Everyone started talking and yelling at once, making Lexi want to crawl into a hole and hibernate. She'd known this wasn't going to be easy, but a free-for-all wasn't what she'd expected, either.

"What the hell are you doing here?" Lexi heard Nash say behind her. Turning, she saw Shane standing by the front door.

"I tried the bell, but I guess no one heard me," Shane said, the room becoming deathly silent. "I take it you told them."

"You knocked up my sister?" Nash stood an inch shorter than Shane but carried slightly more muscle from working on the farm. "Answer me, Langtry."

"I did but—"

Those were the only words Nash needed to hear before he punched Shane in the face, knocking him into the door.

"Nash, what are you doing?" Lexi rushed to Shane's side, blocking her brother from hitting him again. "Are you okay?"

"Oh, that's going to leave a mark." Shane touched the side of his face. "I'd expect no less from you, Nash. I would have done the same thing."

"Get out of this house," Nash growled, pushing Shane through the doorway.

"You get your butt over here." Her mother yanked Shane into the living room. "I want to see the both of you in the kitchen."

Shane leaned into Lexi as they hurriedly walked through the dining room. "You do have ice in there, right?"

Lexi smiled. Levity after being punched in the face was either brave or incredibly stupid and she hadn't quite figured out which one Shane was yet. She was also surprised to see him.

"I don't need help, Nash." Judy swatted behind her. "But good punch, son. As for you two…" Lexi's mother closed the kitchen door. "Sit down."

"I just want to get Shane some—"

"Lexi, sit," Judy ordered. She roughly grabbed hold of Shane's chin and turned his head to the side. "I've seen worse. You'll live…for now."

Removing a small plastic bag from the drawer, Judy filled it with ice, knotted it closed and shoved it at Shane.

"Start from the beginning."

Lexi took a deep breath and felt Shane's fingers intertwine with hers. Somewhere over the past few hours a change of heart had occurred with him and she wasn't about to look a gift horse in the mouth.

Her mother stared at her disbelievingly when she finished her story.

"Will I be able to meet him?" Judy asked. "And be a part of his life?"

"I don't know." Lexi shrugged. "We have to work that out with the Rathbones. Hunter is their child now and we have to play by their rules."

"Don't I have grandparents' rights? I've heard about cases like that."

"So you're planning on suing them?" Lexi smirked. "No judge would try that case, Mom, and I severed all rights when I gave him up. It's not up to us."

"Do you want a relationship with him now?" her mother asked.

"I would like to get to know him better," Lexi admitted. "Do I want to take him away from the only family he knows and loves? Absolutely not."

"I still don't understand why you didn't come to us," Judy said. "We would have helped you. It takes a village to raise a child and the Lawson farm is a small village."

Lexi smiled at her mother's analogy. She knew her mother was right. If she'd told them, she'd have had the baby and they'd have raised it for her, until the Langtrys came in and sued her for custody. There was no way they would have allowed Lexi's parents to raise her child when the father was very much in the picture. It was a scenario she'd considered, but the thought of Sharon anywhere near her child gave her fits of terror. She didn't trust the woman not to harm their baby and Lexi was relieved when Tab won sole custody of Dylan once the paternity results were revealed. Sharon was the type of gold digger you saw on Jerry Springer.

"What about you?" Judy said to Shane. "What do you have to say for yourself?"

"It's brand-new to me, too," Shane said. "I'm hearing this for the first time just like you are."

"You realize if you hadn't screwed up so bad you and my daughter would have raised Hunter together."

"Mother!" Lexi knew her mother was upset with her, but she hadn't expected the cruelty.

"I know I'm responsible, Mrs. Lawson," Shane acknowledged. "I understand now why Lexi did it and

I hope I get the opportunity to spend more time with my son."

"I don't know what's going on between you two again, but let me make myself perfectly clear." Judy leaned over Shane and braced herself on the arm rails of the chair, inches from him. "If you break her heart again, I'll break something of yours and I can promise you it will be more near and dear to you than your heart."

By midnight, they had thoroughly answered all the questions put forth by the Lawson inquisition. Even though she was exhausted, Lexi wanted time alone with Shane to learn more about his meeting with Hunter. He'd mentioned some of it to her mother but she wanted to hear every detail of what their son had to say.

"I guess you need to get home, huh?" Lexi walked Shane out on the front porch.

"Not necessarily. I'm tired and sore." Shane rubbed his jaw. "But I think I'm too wired to sleep at this point."

"I'd ask you to stay here and talk but I'm afraid Nash might shoot you." Lexi feared it was a real possibility. "There's a twenty-four-hour Dunkin' Donuts near the Rathbones' hotel."

"Sure, but we'll take my Jeep." Shane held the door open for her. "No offense but I don't trust your family not to cut my brake lines."

"Good call," Lexi agreed. "Are you okay to drive?"

"You can drive." Shane tossed her the keys.

Lexi had learned not to talk when driving a convertible. The passenger couldn't hear you and you never knew when something was going to fly over the windshield and end up in your mouth. She'd swallowed a fly like that one time. The Jeep was no exception and their ride was silent.

Parking, she pulled the key out of the ignition but made no move to get out. Hunter's hotel was yards away. Inside their son was sleeping. *Their son.*

"Come on," Shane said. "We'll see him in a few hours."

They both ordered coffee and decided to split a small box of Munchkins. At a corner table, they finally had the chance to sit down and absorb the situation.

"Long day?" Shane joked.

"That's putting it mildly," Lexi said. "It's really happening, isn't it?"

Their eyes met and Shane nodded, then reached for her hands. For the second time that night, they linked them together and Lexi started to cry.

"Dammit." She tried to turn her head away from him but he caught her chin. "I never cry. And today I'm all over the map. I'm not saying I regret today because I am so glad it happened, but I keep thinking if I had just stayed away from Family Day this morning, like my gut told me to, none of this would have happened and we'd never have this chance. In a little while Hunter would have returned to Denver and nothing would have changed."

"Well, maybe not for me." Shane wiped the tears from her face. "Could you really have let Hunter go, knowing he was ours?"

Lexi nodded. "I didn't want to hurt or confuse him. I didn't expect his parents to be open to the idea of us spending time with him. Believe it or not, I never wanted to hurt you, either. This wasn't revenge for you cheating on me."

"Hunter told me that his little sister's biological mother...oh, wait, what does he call her? Bonus mom—

his sister's bonus mom has been in touch with her since day one."

"Really?" That gave Lexi hope of a future with Hunter. "How does that work?"

"It was an open adoption. They had agreed to her being a part of Amelia's life from the start and they were fine with it. You're right, they are good people. A little mistrusting of us at the moment, but hopefully after today, they'll realize we had no idea Hunter was ours."

"That's my fault." Lexi pulled apart a chocolate Munchkin and popped half of it in her mouth. "Once I realized who they were, I should have called and told them the truth."

"I tried putting myself in your shoes, and it's difficult to do—being a man and the whole pregnancy thing—you deserved so much better than what I did to you."

"Really?" Lexi was surprised to hear his admission. "I thought you'd always hate me."

"I love you, Lexi," Shane admitted. "I may get mad at you and I can definitely say no woman has ever made me feel shame like you do, but I could never hate you."

Lexi wasn't sure if his words were meant as a friendship "I love you" or if he meant more by the declaration. Tonight it didn't matter. If it was more, she'd hear the words again. If it wasn't, then so be it. This morning she'd lived in fear and under a cloud of secrecy. Tonight, she'd never felt more at peace.

"HE ASKED ABOUT your family," Shane said. Although after tonight's melee, he wasn't sure how much Hunter should be around the Lawsons. They'd probably poison Hunter against him.

"I can just imagine what you told him. My mother hasn't been too nice to you through the years."

"She's just protecting her baby. I understand that." He'd let Judy off the hook for hating him years ago. Once he married Sharon, the woman had every right to hate him. "I told him about the farm and the store, but he's really excited to see the petting zoo."

"He definitely loves animals," Lexi said. "The night your mom and I picked up Barney, he told me he has dogs back home."

"Maybe he'll become a veterinarian when he grows up." Shane smiled, imagining what it would be like to have a doctor for a son.

"I thought you wanted him to ride."

"I do. Hey, he could always be a rodeo vet," Shane laughed. "They do have them, you know."

"I'm well aware of their vet practices, thank you."

"He definitely has your tongue, Sassy Lawson." Shane playfully nudged her arm.

It was nice being able to share something this intimate with Lexi again. Shane wasn't sure how the visitation would work out but he was willing to take anything tossed his way, especially if it meant spending more time with Hunter. Only one week left in class and then their time would end. Shane hoped it wouldn't be long before his son saw him again.

Lexi slid a penny across the table to him and tapped it. He'd forgotten their "penny for your thoughts" game from when they were kids.

"I was just thinking how much I'm going to miss him when he leaves next week. I guess it's really not fair to you."

"What's not?" Lexi asked.

"I get to spend twenty-four hours a day with him and you just see him here and there."

"My punishment, I guess." Lexi smiled. "I'll be fine."

"Aww, don't say that," Shane said. "Maybe we can take a vacation together? All of us, including the Rathbones and their other kids, as a 'getting to know you' type trip. Maybe a cruise?"

"I think the kids would love that," Lexi said. "Maybe we can mention it to them in the morning unless… Do you think they'll think we're trying to buy Hunter's affections?"

"It's a fine line we'll have to be aware of, but I think we can bring it up tactfully."

A few hours and multiple coffees later, they drove out of the parking lot and headed home. Still in the previous day's clothes, they both were in need of showers.

"I'll pick you up around a quarter to eight?" Shane pulled into Lexi's driveway, noticing the curtains in the front window fluttered as he cut the engine. "That gives us a little over two hours."

"That sounds good. Gives me a chance to clean up."

"Let me walk you to the door." Shane unbuckled his seat belt.

Lexi reached out and grabbed his arm. "I wouldn't do that if I were you. Until I talk to Nash, I think you need to stay in the safety of your vehicle, although this thing doesn't offer you much protection."

They both laughed at the thought while keeping an eye out for long barrel shotguns.

"Just for the record, I'm glad this is all out in the open now," Lexi confessed, not releasing her grip on his arm. "It was painfully hard to keep that secret."

"I can imagine it was," Shane said. "No matter what's going on in your life, Lexi, you can always come to me, even if it involves me. I'm sorry for the horrible way I treated you earlier."

Their face inches apart, Shane ran his thumb across Lexi's bottom lip. Her tongue darted out to moisten them. He couldn't resist any longer—overprotective brother be damned, he wanted to kiss her and he *was* going to kiss her.

Cupping her face with one hand, Shane gently tugged her toward him, a barely noticeable effort thanks to her willingness. She reached for his face, carefully avoiding Nash's handiwork. He tasted her gently at first, then quickly she became a need he found almost impossible to resist.

He heard Lexi's breath quicken with each kiss. Every tongue stroke sent his mind in one direction that led south of her border. He forced himself to remember where he was—in front of her house, with her family inside. He had disrespected her once by cheating on her. He wasn't going to do it again by taking things too far in her driveway for her family to see.

Breaking the kiss, he made himself pull away from her. "Not here," he whispered. "I'll be with you anytime, anyplace, but definitely not here."

Lexi nodded and gave him one last lingering kiss goodbye before she jumped from the Jeep and bounded up the porch stairs.

It turned out to be a good night and he had a feeling it was going to be an even better tomorrow.

LEXI QUICKLY LOCKED the front door behind her and ran up the staircase to her bedroom, ignoring the sulking form that sat on the couch waiting up for her. If her mother wanted to sit there in the dark, that was her business, but it didn't mean she had to explain anything. Lexi lived at home out of convenience. Her office and stables were only a few feet away, but whatever happened next with Shane would have to be accepted or she'd find a new place to hang her hat and shingle.

Lexi leisurely showered, washing away the stress of yesterday. She was horrified when she saw her reflection in the mirror and could only imagine what the Rathbones thought of her based on first appearances. Today was a fresh start with Hunter and Shane. She hoped Hunter's parents approved of their cruise idea, but she prepared herself in case they didn't. She expected nothing and was grateful for each and every moment the Rathbones would allow.

The ragtop and doors were on the Jeep when Shane picked her up a few hours later.

"It's an important meeting and I figured you didn't want your hair blowing all over the place. I even cleaned the seats. You look beautiful, by the way."

"Thank you." Lexi loved that Shane remembered how much she hated flowers, candy or anything remotely resembling sappy. His consideration for her hair and her clean seats meant more to her.

"You nervous?" he asked. "Because I sure am. The bruise on the side of my face isn't helping matters."

"I'm definitely nervous," Lexi confessed. So nervous she'd tried on twenty different outfits before settling on a simple coral skirt and a beige fitted T-shirt. "I had a talk with Nash and he promised not to hit you again."

"Does that go for any other weapons or just fists?" Shane joked.

"I think you're safe."

Within minutes, they were in the hotel lobby, waiting

for the Rathbones to come down with Hunter. When the elevator finally opened, Dennis and Melissa appeared but Hunter wasn't with them.

Lexi grabbed Shane's hand and squeezed it. Why wasn't he with them? Had they changed their minds?

It seemed like hours before the couple crossed the room to Lexi and Shane, and Lexi swore she held her breath the entire time.

"We thought we could talk to you both before Hunter came down," Melissa said, zeroing in on their linked hands. "Plus we don't have a babysitter up there for our other two."

Exhaling a sigh of relief, Lexi and Shane followed the Rathbones into the hotel restaurant. This had to be difficult for them, too.

"I see you had a run-in with someone's fist," Dennis said to Shane.

"My brother kind of let him have it last night," Lexi answered for him, knowing no man liked to admit he got his butt kicked.

"You two seem different today." Melissa's tone almost bordered on accusatory. "More couple-like. I didn't get that impression yesterday."

Shane placed his hand over Lexi's on the table. "We're taking things day by day. It's been a whirlwind for us, as I'm sure it has for you and your family."

"It has," Melissa said. "But we're not entirely foreign to this concept. Hunter told us that he explained Amelia's relationship with her birth mother."

"He did and I admire you for supporting that." Shane glanced at Lexi. "We hope someday you will feel the same about us."

"That's what we wanted to discuss," Dennis began,

and Lexi feared they had thought things over and decided not to allow Hunter to see them. "We've heard through others that Hunter has some real talent and we concede to knowing zilch about the rodeo. We're not fans of the sport, so let's get that out of the way. We think it's dangerous and it scares us to death but it's in Hunter's blood, and if this is what he chooses then we're not going to stop him."

"Hunter has expressed interest in attending your next class in August," Melissa said. "And while we would like him home for the second half of the summer, we feel it's important for him to get to know the both of you."

Lexi's mouth dropped open, but she was unable to speak. She looked at Shane, who put his hands over his eyes and half laughed, half cried.

"That's if you have room for him in your next class," Dennis added. "We told him we would check with you first."

"I don't know what to say." Lexi leaned into Shane, resting her head lightly on his shoulder and smiling. "We had something we wanted to run past you."

"First, there is always room for Hunter in any of my classes." Shane looked at Lexi and she nodded, giving him the go-ahead. "I think we might have an idea that would suit everyone's needs. How would you, Hunter and your other children feel about going on a cruise with us before the summer's out? It's our invite, we'd cover all your expenses. And you can even bring Amelia's bonus mom."

"Now I'm the speechless one." Melissa softened slightly, tears in her own eyes. "Honey, we were planning on taking a family trip anyway. What do you think?"

"I think it sounds like a wonderful idea," Dennis said. "But I think Melissa and I need to discuss it further. We're going to go up and get Hunter, and we'll see about the trip."

After spending the next hour talking with Hunter alone, the Rathbones rejoined them and announced they'd decided the trip would be a great way to get to know one another. Lexi was introduced to their other two children and they ate brunch together while they told the kids about the upcoming vacation. Lexi loved the way all three children's faces lit up as they planned the excursions they wanted go on.

The four of them discussed travel plans over coffee and the Rathbones decided since Hunter was staying with Shane on the ranch until the second week in August, they would meet in Walt Disney World for a few days before a ten-day Caribbean cruise.

Hunter rode home with Lexi and Shane, saying goodbye to his parents at the hotel. Lexi gave them a lot of credit. It couldn't have been easy for them to leave their son behind with his biological parents, especially when they had so many unanswered questions.

"You guys are the best!" Hunter said when he climbed in the backseat of the Jeep.

"We think you're pretty special, too," Lexi said.

She felt herself relax for the first time in days. They arrived this morning not knowing how much of their son they would be able to see. They left as a family planning a vacation together. As Hunter would say, *tight!*

Chapter Thirteen

"Lexi!" Shane shouted. "We're going to be late."

Lexi's bedroom window flew open and she popped her head out. "One minute!" She waved to Hunter, who was leaning out of the Lincoln Navigator's side window.

"Don't encourage her, Hunter," Shane chastised. The teen giggled and sat back down in his seat.

"I'm coming, I'm coming." Lexi pushed her way out the front door with two suitcases in tow. "Okay, Mom, I'm leaving," Lexi shouted through the door.

"Have a great time, dear." Judy stepped out on the porch and gave Lexi a hug. Shane loaded the suitcases in the SUV, while Judy said hello to her grandson. "You make sure she behaves, Hunter."

"I will."

"And you." Judy addressed Shane. He guessed it could have been worse. At least she was down to three-letter words instead of four. "Try not to do anything stupid."

"Yes, Mrs. Lawson." Shane struggled not to crack a smile. *Now that would have been stupid.*

"Oh, hello, Chase," Judy said. "I didn't see you there. You drive safely."

Shane held the back door open for Lexi to sit next to Hunter while he sat up front with his brother.

"Judy just loves you to death, doesn't she?" Chase snickered.

"Shut up and drive." Shane laughed.

"Oh, wait!" Lexi called out. "Stop for Nash."

Nash leaned in the window and gave his sister a hug. "Don't worry, I have everything covered here. Enjoy your vacation, sis. I can't remember you ever taking one."

They made it to the airport with only minutes to spare. After saying goodbye to Chase and getting one last reassurance that the school was covered, Shane allowed the excitement of their trip to set in. Despite his extensive traveling, he couldn't remember the last time he went on a nonworking vacation. This was a real treat.

Ironically, the same woman he'd flirted with the day he picked up Hunter waited on them at the ticket counter. He smiled sheepishly, wondering what she thought today as he stood in front of her with a woman and kid. Whatever it was, she only shook her head and they were on their way.

"She seemed to recognize you," Lexi said.

"She gave me a hard time when I picked up Hunter last month." So it was a little white lie.

They boarded the plane moments later.

"Wow, first class!" Hunter exclaimed.

"You are definitely spoiling him." Lexi leaned across the aisle toward Shane's seat. "Me, too, but this time I'll let it go. Just remember, he has another family with a much more modest lifestyle," she added quietly.

"They're flying to Florida first class, too." Shane

smiled. "Stop looking at me like that. It was the least I could do considering everything they've done for us."

"That's all fine and good, but I'm serious, Shane. After this trip, no more extravagances. The Rathbones will end up resenting us."

"Yes, dear."

Shane hated to leave before the August kids completed class. By the time they returned from vacation, his students would be gone. Having to say goodbye to his first class had come with some unexpected emotions. Originally he'd started the rodeo school for profit, but was surprised at how much he enjoyed teaching and being around kids. Even more, he was surprised at how attached he'd grown to each one of them.

While he still wasn't sure where his relationship with Lexi was going, he definitely enjoyed the direction it had begun to take. He'd love to have the chance of children in their future, but today, he was very content with the one they had.

The beginning of this trip was bittersweet. The countdown to when they had to say goodbye to Hunter had officially started. They had two weeks left together and Shane was determined to make the most out of every fun-packed moment. He knew Lexi didn't want to spoil Hunter, but this was a once-in-a-lifetime trip for both families, and their wish was his command. Nothing was off limits.

LEXI SWORE THEY rode every ride at Disney World, Sea World and Universal Studios in three whirlwind days. As kids, she and her siblings always wanted to go to Disney World, but as a farming family, they couldn't afford the trip. The Rathbones, their children and Amelia's bonus mom, Bethany, traveled like normal families on vacation, and with Shane and Lexi, they defined the term *blended family.*

Their ten-day cruise to the Caribbean was breathtaking, and Lexi fulfilled another lifelong dream when she swam with the dolphins during their excursion to Atlantis. Sharing the experience with the two men in her life made it all the more special. And somewhere between Jamaica and St. Martin's, she realized Shane was the man she wanted to spend the rest of her life with.

During their vacation, Lexi and Shane had an opportunity to witness the Rathbones' parenting style. Choosing to leave all discipline up to them, Lexi appreciated their fairness. For the most part, they allowed their children to make their own decisions, within reason.

Melissa presented them with a very liberal holiday schedule, allowing Lexi and Shane to rotate the holidays with them. This year, Hunter would visit them for Thanksgiving and next year for Christmas. Summers were open, allowing Hunter to choose his destination. Melissa and Dennis were being more than generous, and Lexi felt she'd made the right decision thirteen years ago.

Then the day Lexi dreaded had finally arrived. Hunter was flying to Colorado with his family and she was heartbroken. She'd never imagined saying goodbye this time around would hurt this much.

"I had a great time this summer." Hunter fought to hold back his tears. "It was more than I expected. Thank you."

Unable to hold back her own emotion any longer, Lexi cried when she hugged him goodbye. "You are the greatest gift in the world."

"Don't cry, Mom." Hunter wiped her cheeks.

The word she never thought she'd hear was pure heaven. "I've loved you from the moment I knew I was pregnant with you. Please always know that. I love you, Hunter."

"I love you, too. I've had a wonderful life. I wouldn't trade it in for anything and I have you to thank for that."

Hugging her son one last time, she kissed him on the cheek and walked him the final length to the security check point where Shane and the Rathbones waited.

"Thank you for allowing me that time alone with him," Lexi said to Melissa. "I will always be grateful."

Lexi hugged Melissa and the rest of the family before they said their final goodbyes.

"We promise to come see you ride soon," Shane said, clearly not sure if he should hug or shake his son's hand. Hunter made the decision for him when he threw himself into Shane's arms.

"I love you, Dad."

"I love you, too, son."

LEXI SLEPT MOST of their flight home. Shane asked her to stay at the ranch at least for the night, but Lexi said she wanted to sleep in her own bed after sleeping in a strange one for the past two weeks. He knew how much she missed Hunter, because he missed him just as much. What surprised him was Judy's attitude toward him when he dropped Lexi off at the house. She was borderline cordial and Shane wondered if hell had frozen over.

Back home, he walked down the eerily quiet path toward the bunkhouse. The second monthlong class had ended a few days ago and the outbuildings were once again vacant. The ranch seemed empty without the sound of Hunter's laughter and Shane swore if he closed his eyes and listened really carefully, he could still hear his son's voice.

The kid had grown on him even before Shane knew he was his son. He was so proud of him. In two months, Hunter had improved his riding and was ready for the junior rodeo. Shane swore he saw the kid shoot up two inches over the summer. The Rathbones agreed to allow Shane to manage Hunter's career and that guaranteed his rodeo schedule wouldn't be overbooked. He wasn't going to watch Hunter burn out as he'd witnessed so many times with other young rodeo talents. Tomorrow he wanted to start planning some fall events, and Shane planned on being there for every one of them. He knew Lexi's schedule was tight, but he hoped she'd be able to join them on most trips.

When Lexi arrived at the ranch the next morning, Shane noticed she was more quiet than usual, feeling Hunter's absence, too. Shane always thought life was exciting on Bridle Dance, but without the laughter of children, there was no joy in it. He'd make a point to spend extra time with Cole and Tess's daughter, Ever, when she came home from school, and soon Miranda and Jesse's twins would start coming for visits.

The rodeo classes were scheduled for after-school hours and weekends with a few weeklong clinics here and there. Since there were so few people coming and going on the ranch, Shane told Kay to have the Dance of Hope therapists use the front corrals instead of the secluded ones behind the building. It helped hearing children's voices again, but no child could replace his own.

Searching the stables for Lexi, he found her inside

Apollo's stall. Now six weeks old, the colt was frisky and playful and did not appreciate a vet exam. Outwitting Lexi and Ashleigh, Apollo wouldn't allow them to catch him.

"How about you have dinner with me later?" Shane asked.

Ashleigh stopped and wiped the sweat from her face. "I'm sorry, I'm married."

"Just my luck," Shane laughed. "What do you say, doc? The Whole Enchilada for dinner?"

"Ooh, fancy." Lexi nodded. "That actually involves me taking a shower."

LEXI WAS LOOKING forward to a night out even though she was still drained from their trip. The thought of hanging around the house or the ranch doing nothing made her miss Hunter even more. He had video-chatted with her last night when he arrived home, thanking her again for everything. The kid was amazing. Lexi gave him away and he thanked her for it because he loved his life that much.

Now that they were on dry land, the romance of the sea and Hunter gone, Lexi wondered where her relationship with Shane would lead next. The old Shane, the kind and generous one she fell in love with in high school, had reappeared and she hoped he stayed.

Lexi still took Autumn for her afternoon rides, but they were no longer pensive and wrought with angst. Autumn sensed her mood change and began to take more liberties during their outings. Taking off and galloping around the fishing pond had been her latest. Lexi felt good and so did her horse.

She was eager to talk to Shane tonight about a business proposition she'd received this morning from the large animal vet who usually covered her emergency calls. Dr. Rhodes wanted to know if she'd be interested in combining their practices. While she specialized in equine internal health and reproduction, Dr. Rhodes's practice included livestock as well as equine care. There were pros and cons but ultimately it would free up some of her time and allow her to visit Hunter's rodeo events with Shane.

After Lexi showered and changed for her date with Shane, she joined her mother in the kitchen while she prepared the family's dinner.

"How are you doing, Mom?" Lexi gave her a kiss on the cheek.

"Don't you look pretty." Judy motioned for her to spin around. "Night out with the girls?"

Lexi laughed. "You know I'm going to dinner with Shane. I have a few minutes before I have to head over there and I thought I'd spend them with you."

"It's sinful that he doesn't pick you up like a proper lady."

'Well, considering I had his kid out of wedlock at eighteen, I think that negates the whole 'proper lady' thing and Shane doesn't exactly get a warm welcome when he comes here."

"I was very well-behaved yesterday when he dropped you off, wasn't I?"

"I'm still trying to figure that one out." Lexi squinted at her mother. "Either you really missed me or you got into my horse tranquilizers."

"Now, now, respect your elders," Judy said. "Do you think Hunter would mind if I sent him a letter?"

"I think he'd love it, but you'll get better results with

an email instead. And then he can write you back easily. You can call him on video chat if you'd like. I can set you up on the computer or you can use my phone."

"Really, I can see and talk to him?"

"Here, what time is it? He's an hour behind us but he's out of school by now." Lexi pressed the video-chat button on her phone and Hunter's number appeared. "You ready, Mom?"

"What do I do?"

"Hold the phone up in front of you, like this." Lexi held her phone a foot in front of her face and handed it back to her mother. "Are you ready to call him?"

Judy eagerly nodded, her excitement evident.

"Press this button." Lexi pointed to the big green *send.*

After two rings, Hunter answered, his beautiful blue eyes looking back at them.

"Hi." Hunter waved.

"He waved…did you see that?"

"Yes, Mom, I saw. It's on speakerphone. Talk to him, not me."

"Hey, Mom, where are you?" Hunter asked.

"I'm here, honey. Trying to teach this one how to video-chat."

"Wicked," Hunter said.

"How was your first day of school?" Judy asked.

"It was all right. I'm in a new school this year so I have to learn where everything is."

"Why is he in a new school?" Judy asked Lexi.

"Because he's in eighth grade." Lexi pointed to the screen. "Ask Hunter, not me. He sees you talking to me."

"Oh." Judy looked back at the phone. "You know, Hunter, I've never been to Colorado. Maybe I can fly out and see one of your events with Lexi and Shane. Would that be okay?"

"That would be awesome. Is Grandpa Jim going to come, too?"

"Oh, you want him there?" Judy frowned. "I kind of wanted to leave him home."

"Mother." Lexi swatted her. "Let me talk to him." She took the phone from Judy. "Hey, sweetie. Did your first day really go okay? You seem down."

"Yeah, I just hate being in the youngest class." Hunter made a face. "We're the babies. You look real pretty. Are you going out?"

"Shane's taking me to dinner at the Whole Enchilada."

"You know he's in love with you, don't you?"

"How do you know that?" Lexi asked, wondering if her mother overheard his comment. Glancing back, Lexi saw she had returned to cooking dinner.

"A man senses these things about another man."

"Does he?" Lexi smiled, loving every moment she could talk to her son whether on a tiny screen or in person.

"Yeah, well, that and the fact he talks about you nonstop. I'm surprised he didn't drown when we were snorkeling because he rambled on so much."

"You're making that up."

"Maybe the drowning part but not the rest," Hunter said. "I like seeing you two together. He was grumpy without you."

"That's what people said about me," Lexi added.

"I know." Hunter giggled. "I always heard that Lexi Lawson is the grumpiest person around."

"You are so going to get it." Lexi laughed.

SHANE'S PHONE RANG while he waited for Lexi to arrive that evening. His agent's name appeared on the display.

"Give me the good news," Shane said.

"You got it," Brock said, sounding less than enthused

"Woo-hoo!" Shane shouted.

"The network wants to buy it and start filming next month. They chose five rodeo cowboys but I don't know who the others are. We may not find out until after they start filming. Adds the element of reality TV surprise."

"Before you go any further," Shane began. "Hold up for a minute. There's something I want to tell you. Brock, you're never going to believe this, but I have a son."

"Is that why you've been unreachable for the past few weeks? You really should keep your agent in the loop, so I don't keep telling people I *might* be able to book you for an appearance. Who'd you knock up this time?"

"Hey, now, it's not like that and that wasn't even true back then," Shane argued. "Well, actually it was but I didn't know it."

"Dylan's really your son?"

"Not Dylan." Shane stepped out on the front porch overlooking the walnut trees lining the main entrance. "Hunter Rathbone. Remember that name because this kid is going to be a megastar. He has all my talent and his mother's brains—"

"How old is this kid that he's so talented?" Brock interrupted.

"He just turned thirteen." Shane saw Lexi's black Mustang convertible turn down the road, clouds of dust kicking up behind her. He walked back into the house to grab the junior rodeo schedule printouts.

"You're not thinking about putting him on the show,

are you?" Brock asked. "Because I don't think that's the *adult* angle they're going for."

"Adult?" Shane asked. "What are you talking about? This is something my kid can watch, isn't it?"

"Of course, although I'm still baffled by this kid thing. It won't be X-rated, but I warned you about these types of shows, especially with Keeping it Reel Pictures. Sex sells and I'm sure they'll plant groupies for your viewing pleasure."

Lexi walked through the side door. She was gorgeous in her denim shorts and mile-long legs still tan from their cruise. Normally in boots or sneakers, she wore wedge-heeled sandals that tied at the ankle and a white flowing short-sleeve shirt. Her dark mahogany hair fell in long, loose waves down her back. When she removed her sunglasses, her eyes met his and she smiled. He'd waited a lifetime for that smile and now it was his. This was his viewing pleasure.

"It's not going to work," Shane said to Brock.

"What's not going to work? Are you talking to me or someone else?"

"I'm talking to you. Please tell them thanks, but no thanks."

Before Brock could argue, Shane disconnected the call and crossed the room to Lexi.

"What was that all about?" Lexi said, looking down on the counter. "Are these Hunter's upcoming rodeo dates?"

"Mmm-hmm." Shane wrapped his arms around Lexi and pulled her body against his. "And that was Brock telling me the network wants to buy the show and start filming next month."

"I don't understand. I heard you say 'no thanks.'"

Lexi's confusion was evident in her furrowed brow and wrinkled nose. "I thought this is what you wanted."

"You're right." Shane spread his legs slightly, fitting her tighter to him. "*This* is what I want. You, right here in front of me."

Shane took her mouth with his. There was no pretense, no gentleness. It was a kiss meant to speak for him. A strong, passionate kiss that she relented to and responded in kind. Cupping her bottom, he lifted her as she wrapped her legs around his waist. Carrying her upstairs and into his bedroom, he kicked the door closed with his foot.

Laying her on the bed, he stepped away and moved toward the window, leaving her to whimper.

"I told Brock no," Shane said.

Dazed, her lips swollen from his kisses, she propped herself up on her elbows.

"You told who, what?"

He crossed the room and stood at the foot of the bed. The woman he loved was ready and willing for him. A more beautiful sight didn't exist. He wanted to kiss her and make love to her, but he had something more important to tell her first.

"I told Brock that I'm not doing the reality show." Shane reached for her hand, pulling her into an upright position. "I realized it doesn't mean the same to me anymore."

"Why the change of heart?" Lexi asked.

"Our son and you." Shane held her hand in his. "I don't want to do it anymore. I'd rather focus on us, the school and the ranch, and honestly, being the center of attention is really draining."

"What about the rodeo?" Lexi questioned.

"I'll still ride in some events but I'm going to scale way back. Let this be Chase's year." Cutting back wasn't part of the plan until he won the championship. "He doesn't have the commitments I do and this leaves a lot more time open for me to see Hunter."

"I can't believe what I'm hearing," Lexi said. "Dr. Rhodes asked me if I wanted to combine practices. I haven't decided one way or the other, but it would free me up more, too."

"That would be incredible," Shane said. He leaned in for a kiss and tugged her to the edge of the bed so her legs hung off the edge. "There's something I want to talk to you about."

"Should I be worried?" Lexi grimaced.

"I hope not," Shane said. "Let me ask you this— where do you see us going?"

"I'm not sure," Lexi admitted. "I love being with you and I love being with our son. These past two months have been wild and crazy and they define us perfectly. Why?"

"The way I see it, you and I are meant to be." Shane lowered himself on one knee. "We had a rough go of it no thanks to me, but our love for one another created a pretty incredible kid."

"Shane, what are you doing?"

"We are always going to be a part of one another's lives and I can't think of another woman I'd want to share my life with. I've done a lot of thinking, I know you're not the ring kind of girl, especially with where you stick your hands, and my job's no better in that regard. So, I say we screw tradition, get ourselves hitched, tattoo a couple of wedding rings on our fingers and do this. What do you say? Will you marry me?"

IF THAT WASN'T the most unorthodox proposal she ever heard, Lexi didn't know what was. But it was honest and was Shane being true to himself, and that meant something to her. The past was unchangeable, but the future was wide-open. They had already become an unconventional family thanks to the Rathbones' generosity.

There was no further doubt in her mind—Shane Langtry, the wild rebel of Ramblewood, finally had his own legacy in his son.

"Yes," Lexi laughed. "Now let's do this thing before someone gets wind of it and tries to stop it, namely my brother."

By sunrise, Lexi found herself seated next to Shane on a plane to Las Vegas with Bridgett and Clay across the aisle from them. She didn't think she'd ever get through the ceremony without dying of laughter when an Elvis impersonator at the Graceland Chapel officiated their wedding.

Lexi knew neither family would bat an eye at their elopement. This was their style, and when she looked into Shane's eyes while a burly woman named Wild Jill tattooed a simple band around her ring finger, she knew it was all meant to be.

Shane Langtry was officially a marked man—her man.

* * * * *

#1489 THE TEXAS WILDCATTER'S BABY
McCabe Homecoming
by Cathy Gillen Thacker

Environmentalist Rand McCabe embarks on a passionate affair with lady wildcatter Ginger Rollins, but can't convince her to begin a real relationship with him...until she finds herself unexpectedly pregnant with his child.

#1490 MOST ELIGIBLE SHERIFF
Sweetheart, Nevada
by Cathy McDavid

Ruby McPhee switches places with her twin sister so she can lay low in Sweetheart, Nevada. She doesn't expect complications—except it turns out Ruby is "dating" Cliff Dempsey, local sheriff and the town's most eligible bachelor!

#1491 AIMING FOR THE COWBOY
Fatherhood
by Mary Leo

An unexpected pregnancy hog-ties Helen Shaw's rodeo career and friendship with future father Colt Granger. The sexy cowboy's proposal sounds sweet, but is it the real deal?

#1492 ROPING THE RANCHER
by Julie Benson

Colt Montgomery has sworn off women after his ex left him to raise his teenage daughter alone. When actress Stacy Michaels shows up at his ranch, she tests his resolve to steer clear of women!

REQUEST YOUR FREE BOOKS!
2 FREE NOVELS PLUS 2 FREE GIFTS!

HARLEQUIN

American ★ Romance®

LOVE, HOME & HAPPINESS

YES! Please send me 2 FREE Harlequin® American Romance® novels and my 2 FREE gifts (gifts are worth about $10). After receiving them, if I don't wish to receive any more books, I can return the shipping statement marked "cancel." If I don't cancel, I will receive 4 brand-new novels every month and be billed just $4.74 per book in the U.S. or $5.24 per book in Canada. That's a savings of at least 14% off the cover price! It's quite a bargain! Shipping and handling is just 50¢ per book in the U.S. and 75¢ per book in Canada.* I understand that accepting the 2 free books and gifts places me under no obligation to buy anything. I can always return a shipment and cancel at any time. Even if I never buy another book, the two free books and gifts are mine to keep forever.

154/354 HDN F4YN

Name	(PLEASE PRINT)

Address	Apt. #

City	State/Prov.	Zip/Postal Code

Signature (if under 18, a parent or guardian must sign)

Mail to the **Harlequin® Reader Service:**
IN U.S.A.: P.O. Box 1867, Buffalo, NY 14240-1867
IN CANADA: P.O. Box 609, Fort Erie, Ontario L2A 5X3

**Want to try two free books from another line?
Call 1-800-873-8635 or visit www.ReaderService.com.**

* Terms and prices subject to change without notice. Prices do not include applicable taxes. Sales tax applicable in N.Y. Canadian residents will be charged applicable taxes. Offer not valid in Quebec. This offer is limited to one order per household. Not valid for current subscribers to Harlequin American Romance books. All orders subject to credit approval. Credit or debit balances in a customer's account(s) may be offset by any other outstanding balance owed by or to the customer. Please allow 4 to 6 weeks for delivery. Offer available while quantities last.

Your Privacy—The Harlequin® Reader Service is committed to protecting your privacy. Our Privacy Policy is available online at www.ReaderService.com or upon request from the Harlequin Reader Service.

We make a portion of our mailing list available to reputable third parties that offer products we believe may interest you. If you prefer that we not exchange your name with third parties, or if you wish to clarify or modify your communication preferences, please visit us at www.ReaderService.com/consumerschoice or write to us at Harlequin Reader Service Preference Service, P.O. Box 9062, Buffalo, NY 14269. Include your complete name and address.

HAR13R

Ruby McPhee is hiding out in Sweetheart, Nevada, having changed places with her twin sister. What her sister didn't tell her is that Scarlett was dating the town sheriff! But what happens after Cliff Dempsey figures this out? Find out in MOST ELIGIBLE SHERIFF by Cathy McDavid.

Picking up the bouquet, Cliff said, "These are for you."

"Thanks." Scarlett accepted the flowers and, with both hands full, set them back down on the table. "You didn't have to."

"They're a bribe. I was hoping you'd go with me to the square dance Friday night."

The community center had finally reopened nearly a year after the fire. The barbecue and dance were in celebration.

"I…um…don't think I can. I appreciate the invitation, though."

"Are you going with someone else?" He didn't like the idea of that.

"No, no. I'm just…busy." She clutched her mug tightly between both hands.

"I'd really like to take you." Fifteen minutes ago he probably wouldn't have put up a fight and would have accepted her loss of interest. Except he was suddenly more interested in her than before. "Think on it overnight."

"O-kay." She took another sip of her coffee. As she did, the cuff of her shirtsleeve pulled back.

He saw it then, a small tattoo on the inside of her left wrist resembling a shooting star. A jolt coursed through him. He hadn't seen the tattoo before.

Because seven days ago, when he and Scarlett ate dinner at the I Do Café, it hadn't been there.

"Is that new?" He pointed to the tattoo.

Panic filled her eyes. "Um…yeah. It is."

Cliff didn't buy her story. There were no tattoo parlors in Sweetheart and, to his knowledge, she hadn't left town. And why the sudden panic?

Scarlett averted her face. She was hiding something.

Leaning down, he smelled her hair, which reminded him of the flowers he'd brought for her. It wasn't at all how Scarlett normally smelled.

Something was seriously wrong.

He scrutinized her face. Eyes, chocolate-brown and fathomless. Same as before. Hair, thick and glossy as mink's fur. Her lips, however, were different. More ripe, more lush and incredibly kissable.

He didn't stop to think and simply reacted. The next instant, his mouth covered hers.

She squirmed and squealed and wrestled him. Hot coffee splashed onto his chest and down his slacks. He let her go, but not because of any pain.

"Are you crazy?" she demanded, her breath coming fast.

Holding on to the wrist with the new tattoo, he narrowed his gaze. "Who the hell are you? And don't bother lying, because I know you aren't Scarlett McPhee."

Look for MOST ELIGIBLE SHERIFF *by Cathy McDavid next month from Harlequin® American Romance®!*